VINEYARD SECRETS

Wendy VanHatten

VINEYARD SECRETS

DocUmeant *Publishing*
244 5th Avenue
Suite G-200
NY, NY 10001
646-233-4366
www.DocUmeantPublishing.com

Vineyard Secrets

Hidden Truth Series, Vol. 2

Published by
DocUmeant Publishing
244 5th Avenue, Suite G-200
NY, NY 10001

Phone: 646-233-4366

Copy Editor Corie Barloggi

Cover Design and Layout Ginger Marks

DocUmeantDesigns.com

Printed in The United States of America

ISBN13: 978-1-937801-47-2
ISBN10: 1-937801-47-0

Dedication

To Rick . . . for encouragement and, of course, for introducing me to Prosecco.

Acknowledgments

Many thanks to Corie for her editing, suggestions, and patience; to all those who read the manuscript and gave me feedback; to my dad for giving me the traveling and writing bug; and for all of you who read this.

Prologue

"Be careful . . . be very careful."

Whispered to me with total clarity, an intense look on her face, and my hand held in her strong grip, Grandma's words were clear. Very clear. Then, once more her eyes slowly closed.

Looking around, it appeared no one else heard her. It was almost like they were ignoring some old, dying person uttering mindless words. After all, she was lying in a hospital bed, hooked up to a bunch of different monitors . . . and probably didn't have long to live. But, that didn't mean we should ignore her. And, it definitely didn't mean she was crazy.

To me, her whisper was a warning. And, this was crystal clear. She looked right at me when she said it. The way she gripped my hand was like she used to when I was a little girl and we saw a snake on our walks. I remember how we were both terrified of snakes. This wasn't a casual, flimsy hand shake of a dying, almost lifeless woman, either. It was a real grip, almost a grip of fear.

Like they had been for the last hour, her eyes fluttered open and shut. Then, once again she lay perfectly still . . . so still I had to check the monitor to make sure she was still breathing.

No one seemed to be the slightest bit interested in her. But, then again they didn't know her like I did.

Still holding her now relaxed hand, my brain tried to grasp what she had just told me . . . actually warned me. What did Grandma mean? What should I be careful of, anyway? Why did she look right at me, almost right through me? I looked around. Why didn't anyone else notice what just happened?

Talking in hushed voices, everyone else in the room was more focused on other things than this sweet old woman lying in the hospital bed. Not one of them appeared to be concerned that Grandma was slowly slipping away. In fact, I'm not quite sure what all these people were doing here. Who were they, anyway?

One guy looked totally out of place as he walked by Grandma. He appeared to survey the entire group as he peered out from under his hat. When he caught me looking at him, he quickly and silently left the room.

Perhaps I should go after him and ask if he is related or if he knows my grandma. Just then she stirred ever so slightly in the bed. I'll ask someone about him later . . .

Lovingly looking back at her, I smiled as this time she widely opened her soft, blue eyes and gave me the secret wink we used when we wanted to avoid my mother. It was our special code, and when I was a little girl it always made me feel like a co-conspirator in some thriller.

As I leaned in to kiss her cheek, she whispered "It's in the cookbook. Don't let anyone else have it. People will try to steal them. They are all yours now." It? Them? What, Grandma, what?

I started to ask what she meant but it was too late.

Sighing softly, she let out her last breath. I knew she was gone. I could feel it. Soft tears fell from my eyes as I kissed her paper thin cheek for the last time.

Chapter 1

Grandma is gone but I have my memories.

Memories . . . so many wonderful memories of Grandma swirl around in my mind as I sit here thinking in the silence. Soon that silence will be broken as relatives, friends, and acquaintances fill up this church. I have no doubt it will be bursting at the seams . . . Grandma knew a lot of people. She had touched a lot of hearts in her long life as well.

I wanted these few moments of solitude with her before I was overwhelmed with everyone's condolences. Grandma's wishes were adhered to, all the arrangements were made, and I was in charge . . . just like she wanted. She would have a closed casket funeral and absolutely no flowers. "Flowers are for the living," she used to tell me. "And close the lid. I don't want anyone to see me in that box. If they wanted to see an old woman, they should have visited me when I was alive." She was vocal and quite adamant about her wishes. I smiled in remembrance.

After the memorial service, she was to be cremated. Sometime within the next year I was to carry her ashes back to Italy. I haven't had time to figure out that part just yet. With all the rules and regulations about air travel and ashes . . . I may have to get creative.

In her true Grandma form, she had everything all mapped out for me; where she wanted her ashes scattered and how I was to get there. We talked in depth about her wishes in the last year. Actually, we joked about me carrying her ashes, tripping, and scattering them on an old, Italian cobblestone pathway. She laughed and laughed at the site of me trying to sweep up her ashes and put them back in the urn. At first, I didn't think it was funny. But, the more she exaggerated the scene, the more she laughed and laughed. I couldn't help but to laugh along with her.

Normally, all the arrangements would have been handled by Dad as Grandma was his mother. But, that wasn't to be. Almost twenty five years ago Mom and Dad were on a research trip in South America when their small plane went down supposedly somewhere in the jungle along the Amazon River. The wreckage was never discovered. It's hard to believe it's been that long ago. Wow. I'm not sure I remember much about Mom or Dad or that incident, and Grandma never elaborated on it. I would have been a senior in college. Amazing to think of that now.

For as long as I can remember, Mom and Dad were flying here or there to do some type of research, participate in an archaeological dig, write papers on climate change in the Antarctic, or find artifacts that had been buried by some volcano. As they were both esteemed university professors and valued researchers, it was just the way I grew up. I wasn't close to my parents.

With all the time we spent together, Grandma was my real family. That's why I have so many fantastic memories of her.

Smiling, I remember spending summers on the farm with Grandma and Grandpa while Mom and Dad were off researching the effects of overfishing in the Arctic . . . or something. Grandpa would milk cows and I would steal some milk for all the begging momma cats and kittens. He would role his eyes at me and smile. Grandma let me bring as many kittens in the house as I could carry. Mom didn't want them at home, so I made good use of my time at Grandma's house.

After Grandpa died, Grandma and I spent months cleaning up the farm and selling everything. Because the farm was too much for her to take care of, she bought a smaller house in the city close to ours. One priority I had . . . she had to bring at least a couple of kittens with her. She loved those kittens as much as I did.

One priority she had . . . a state-of-the-art kitchen. She was an accomplished pastry chef who tried out new recipes at home. Then, two days a week she baked her perfected recipes at a local restaurant, creating treats that were always in demand.

Born and raised in Italy, Grandma adopted the United States as her home when she and Grandpa married and moved to Minnesota after World War II. She always said Minnesota winters were just like winters in northern Italy . . . only worse.

As a little girl, I loved listening to her stories about Italy, how she and Grandpa met, how she learned to bake, and so many more, all from long ago. As I became older, I understood the struggles she had growing up in Italy during World War II. Her stories of Venice became my favorites. To this day Venice holds a special place in my heart. We were planning a trip there together . . . and now that won't happen.

I think about how she loved coming to visit me when I moved to San Francisco after college. We would spend time wandering the North Beach neighborhood in the city. We made quite a pair. I am tall, blonde, fair, and can only speak a few Italian words; grazie being one of them. Grandma, on the other hand was short, her dark hair graying ever so slightly, and spoke fluent Italian as well as a special Venetian dialect of Italian. However, one thing we had in common as we chatted our way through cappuccinos and wine . . . neither of us could talk without waving our hands around.

The predominately Italian area of North Beach brought back memories of Italy for her and she slipped right into fluent Italian as she conversed with restaurant owners, bakers, and locals. She had friends on every block and in every shop and restaurant. I remember them all asking me when my grandma was coming to visit. They loved her and I'm sure the feeling was mutual.

Time to quit reflecting for now, as people start to quietly enter the church. Smiling, I head toward the open doors to greet everyone.

Chapter 2

Finally, I'm back in San Francisco, sitting in my living room as the sun works its way into my windows, and reflecting on the last couple of months. Cleaning out Grandma's house after the funeral, working through the legalese with her attorney, dealing with the bank, and putting everything in order the way she wanted wasn't as daunting and overwhelming as I first feared, though.

Things that I knew weren't special to her were sold at a household auction. Unbeknownst to me, Grandma had previously organized the things she wanted me to have, neatly packed them all into shipping boxes, and labeled them to be sent to me after she died. She knew she wouldn't live forever. But, it was almost like she didn't want anyone but me to even see her things. So, some decisions I was afraid I would have to make were already made by Grandma before she died.

Her house sold quickly and all the necessary paperwork finalized in record time. Two weeks after the funeral, Grandma's attorney contacted me and set a time for the reading of her will. I already knew I was the executor but had no idea about any of the rest of the contents in her will.

I think back to sitting in his office, listening to the instructions in her will. Boy, did I learn some things I didn't know about my grandmother. Her attorney and I were seated in his comfortable office, his assistant took notes as we talked and sipped incredible coffee.

First, her will mentioned Mario, a grandson of a chef in Italy. Grandma left a fair amount of money to Mario . . . with the caveat that he must find me and talk to me. Okay. Funny she never mentioned him to me before. Her attorney is to contact him to let him know of her death and then Mario will supposedly contact me. Since she included what appears to be a recent address, she must have been in contact with him on a regular basis.

Huh! Never in all these years did anyone, especially Grandma, mention the name Mario. I guess I have no choice but to wait for his call.

Also in her will she included a fair amount of detail about a special cookbook I need to find in one of her boxes. She explained that once I find it, there will be specific instructions in it for me. She knew I enjoyed cooking and would love to have any of her cookbooks. Hopefully, they are written in English! But, I still don't understand the part about instructions and what they will tell me. When I questioned the attorney . . . he said he only knew what she had in her will. She didn't elaborate.

Sitting here now with thoughts of cookbooks . . . could this be the cookbook she whispered about before she died in the hospital? I had sort of forgotten about that comment and hadn't thought to mention it to the attorney. Maybe Grandma had developed a special, secret recipe. I try to remember exactly what she said to me. It seems it was something about people wanting to steal something from that cookbook. Thinking to myself, it could be recipes . . . maybe.

Her attorney also gave me instructions for some charities. I knew Grandma contributed to several charities and participated on some boards. She included that list in her will, with the suggestion I continue on her behalf. I nodded as he handed me the list.

Next items she mentioned were her wedding ring and some jewelry, which apparently are both included in the boxes already shipped to me. Her instructions specified that I am to have all of it appraised before I did anything with it. I wondered why. Her attorney didn't know that, either. I really wasn't aware Grandma had any special or valuable jewelry, other than her plain gold wedding band.

Finally, she left the rest of her estate to me.

And, I about fell off my chair when the attorney read the amount to me. Grandma and I had never talked seriously about money. From time to time I would ask her if she was doing okay financially. She always told me she had enough for a rainy day and that I wasn't to worry about her. Even though she came to visit me in San Francisco several times a year, she never let me pay for her airplane fare. She was a very proud person and liked to take care of me.

Now I know why. My grandmother was wealthy. Not multi-millionaire wealthy . . . but pretty close to it.

Grandma's estate is settled. Now, I'll have to think about the money and what to do with it.

First though, I need to deal with these boxes sitting here in my living room. I had no idea she had so many things she thought I should have. After all, I thought I had been through all of her stuff more than once. We cleaned out the farmhouse and we sorted everything when she moved into town. What could Grandma possibly have for me?

First, I need a cup of coffee. Then I'll tackle these boxes.

Chapter 3

Shadow, my big, fluffy kitty, is playing hide and seek amongst the boxes as I sit here, drink my morning coffee, and remember Grandma. With one look to the Heavens and a silent prayer to Grandma for guidance, I decide it's time to get in gear and do something with all of these boxes.

If I remember correctly, I have a dinner party scheduled for this weekend. With some new clients and old friends coming to dinner, I really don't need the living room cluttered with boxes. It's a good thing I work as an independent travel consultant and can take time to deal with all of this. Throughout the past couple of months I have been able to schedule my work in amongst dealing with Grandma's death. Now, it's time to seriously get back to work.

It shouldn't take me long to go through all of these, decide what to keep, and figure out what to do with the rest of her things I don't need. Honestly, I don't know how there could be that much more here that she really wanted me to have. Every time she came to visit in the past few months, she brought something of hers to give me.

Reflecting on her last few months, I am so glad she didn't suffer any more than she did the last couple of days in the hospital.

At 95, she was fairly healthy and always the most positive person I knew. Never did she talk about anything negative.

Her stories were full of fun, or tales of how she worked in a hospital cooking and baking for the Allies during WWII, or how she and Grandpa met. Now and then she would talk about a chef who taught her to bake and about a treasure map she and the chef's son made. Whenever I would press her about the treasure map, she would tell me, "It's safe now. When the time is right, you will get to see it. But, for now we must not mention it to anyone."

Then she would change the subject and no amount of coaxing would get her to speak about it again. One time, I did mention it to my parents. My mother told me it was just an old woman's way of telling tall tales. Dad seemed interested and asked if I had seen it. When I told him no, he shrugged it off and told me it was crazy nonsense. I never mentioned it again to anyone. I didn't want my grandma to be thought of as crazy. And, I certainly didn't want her to know I had said anything about it to my parents!

Okay, enough reminiscing. I really must go through all of these boxes. Shadow seems to want to help. He already has clawed through the tape at the end of one of them. I'll start with that one.

Chapter 4

Jumping in and out of partially filled boxes, Shadow loves the game in my living room. So far, we've made it through six of the 10 boxes discovering pieces of Grandma's life. Honestly, I had no idea she had these things and I don't have a single clue where she had kept them all these years. I thought I had been through every inch of her house, both as a kid and later as an adult. I decide to label the boxes in case I need to refer to one of them.

Box one was full of diaries, starting with Grandma as a little girl growing up in northern Italy. Since the early ones are all written in Italian, I'll have to see about getting those translated. It will be interesting to read about her childhood and early years. I wonder if this is why she kept giving me diaries and journals and encouraged me to write when I was younger.

Skimming through these, I notice as her life progressed into her late teen years, she writes in both Italian and English. Her English is amazing and her life easy to follow as she talks about learning the art of pastry making from a chef in Venice. It appears the chef was teaching his son at the same time. Thank goodness each diary is labeled and dated. There are diaries about WW II, about meeting Grandpa, about some strange woman from the village her mother knew, and even one completely devoted to maps.

I put the entire box of diaries in my office where I can sit and piece together Grandma's life later.

Boxes two, three, and four are filled with kitchen tools and gadgets. She has marked everything with a year and how she used that item. Since she mostly made pastries, it appears I now have every baking pan known to man. Throw in several dozen different shapes of cutters, rollers, and pastry bags and I have more gadgets than I will ever use. My apartment is decent size but I have no idea where all of this will go. For now, these boxes stay in one of the guest bedrooms.

Opening boxes five and six, I discover photos. Thankful that Grandma was organized, I see she has them labeled by year and by city. Setting these to the side, I decide I want to look at these while I eat dinner.

Box number seven is full of maps . . . again labeled and organized. Most are old, really old. Some are crumbling as I try to unfold them. Glancing at a couple, I notice she has notes on them. One of the notes refers to a legend or a key and says important. Guess I need to look for that before I try to decipher the maps. This box joins the one with the photos. If I have time, I'll look at these while I eat dinner also.

Opening box number eight, I find a large, stately looking, cherry wood jewelry box. Carefully easing the heavy, cumbersome reddish brown box from its packing box takes some finesse. Finally wrestling it out, I manage to get it to the coffee table and see the key taped to the bottom. Inserting the key into the tiny hole produces a distinctive click and the top slowly rises. Oh . . . my . . . God. I swear my living room just became brighter as all these jewels wink at me. Even Shadow seems mesmerized by the glow.

Where on earth did she get all of this jewelry? I love all gold and sparkly jewelry . . . must have inherited that from her. But, this is more than just a few nice pieces. I have never seen anything like these and have no idea where to start. Is it real?

Probably so, because she left instructions in her will for me to have it appraised. But, what do I say to a jeweler? "I just happened to have found these." That seems lame. I think I'll call my attorney first. Maybe he can give me some direction or at least a place to start.

Deciding to look more closely at some of it, I pick up the first piece that caught my eye . . . a robin's egg blue stone set in a ring. No ordinary ring, this stone is at least the size of a quarter and it seems to change color as the light hits it. Whom did it belong to? Never in all these years did I see Grandma wearing anything like this.

Carefully placing it back in its spot, I reach for a fantastic looking yellow stone on a delicate gold chain.

The doorbell rings, Shadow jumps in an empty box, and I almost screamed. I was so engaged in looking at the jewelry, everything else seemed to disappear.

Chapter 5

Quickly closing the lid and placing the brown shipping box on top of the jewelry box, I head to the door as the bell chimes again. Glancing back to my coffee table, I can see the box isn't really concealed. Why do I think it needs to be hidden?

Once more the doorbell rings as I yank open the door. A delivery man, with an impatient look on his face and a ball cap pulled down on his forehead, hands me an envelope. "Thought no one was home," he says while looking past me into the foyer. "Are you moving?" When I just nod, he shoves a hand held computer to me and says "Please sign here."

Taking the envelope, I start to shut the door. He stays put and says, "Looks like you've got some nice stuff. Keep your door locked." Mystified, again I just nod as I shut and lock the door.

What? Why am I taking instructions from a delivery guy? And, how does he know I have nice stuff?

Shadow jumps out of his hiding spot and rubs up against my leg. "Well, that was the strangest delivery I've ever taken," I mutter to Shadow. Apparently understanding me, he looks up and meows.

Laying the envelope on an end table, I return to the magnificent jewelry box, open it, and just stare at its contents. With each in their own velvet-lined space, seven fairly large brooches adorned with varying gemstones smile up at me. Some have round, faceted stones and some have tiny, sparkly stones. There are reds, greens, blues, and whites . . . all shiny and nestled in their gold filigree of each brooch.

Removing each piece, I carefully set them one by one on the coffee table. Although I love jewelry, I'm not an expert. Still, this certainly doesn't look like costume jewelry. It looks old. But, then again, what do I know? They are all different yet similar in style. One of the brooches looks like it could have an initial or family crest in the design.

Then there are the rings. Each placed in their own velvet ring holder; ten rings with varying stones sit waiting for me to try them on. Most of the rings contain large stones surrounded by smaller ones. You couldn't exactly call them gaudy. But, they don't look like you'd wear them to the grocery store, either. The blue one that caught my eye is by far the most interesting to me. As I hold it up in the light it seems to change color, picking up different shades of blue as the sun hits it. From Caribbean blue to soft robin's egg blue . . . it's a unique ring. Slipping it on my finger makes me feel so special. Are these really mine? I notice it has a matching necklace. What a pair these are.

They all sparkle as I move the tray of rings to the coffee table next to the brooches. All fascinate Shadow who paws at each one. Then, he's off to chase the reflection on the wall as the sun catches the facets of the stones.

Finally, there are three more necklaces, each with a single large stone hanging from a delicate gold chain. One oval stone is almost transparent yellow in color. I've never seen a stone this color. Another one is a distinctive square cut emerald so green it reminds me of a Christmas tree in color. The third one is definitely a sapphire. Its deep blue color couldn't be mistaken for anything else. All are good sized . . . slightly smaller than a quarter. And, all are absolutely brilliant in their clarity.

What a collection. It's breathtaking. Staring at everything on my coffee table, there's really no other word for these jewels than . . . WOW.

Looking back at the jewelry box, I see there is another shelf underneath. Flipping the top shelf up reveals the contents at the bottom of the box. By now, I should expect shiny and fabulous. But . . .

This is beyond wow. I feel like I'm in the vault of some high end jeweler. What on earth did Grandma do with all of this? Better question . . . where did she get this? And, why did she keep it a secret from me? I didn't think we had any secrets from each other.

Carefully lifting out each piece from the bottom, the collection on my coffee table grows.

Now I have seven more necklaces. Only these are not on delicate gold chains. The multiple stones with ornate gold work hang from substantial gold ropes made up of intertwining links. Each one is considerably heavier than the ones on the top shelf. These almost look regal in nature . . . not dainty by any means. You wouldn't just wear these to a casual cocktail party or informal dinner. These were definitely meant for showing off on some ball gown. They are that stunning.

In addition, there are four cuff style bracelets . . . all gold with stones embedded in them.

My goodness . . . this is overwhelming to say the least.

Chapter 6

Carefully placing everything back in the jewelry box, I realize I have two more unopened packing boxes. Am I ready for these?

Opening box I labeled number nine reveals yet another jewelry box. Or, at least I think it's a jewelry box. It's not as large as the last one, but heavy for its size. Running my hand over the smooth top, the workmanship and detail of the white, black, and gold inlaid designs is incredible. This must be mother of pearl as iridescent as it is. The whole top depicts a scene from Venice . . . gondolas, canals, and stately buildings.

Again, a small key is taped to the bottom of the box . . . this time with a note. Unfolding the paper the words 'ask Mario about these' are written in English. No time like the present to see what these are. Inserting the key, I open the lid and stare at two small boxes. Jewels of varying sizes cover their tops. The rest of the boxes appear to be gold or gold plated . . . who knows at this point? Removing one of these I see it's actually a music box.

Placing it on my coffee table, I gently open the lid and music fills my living room. Not recognizing the tune or the composer, I close that lid and reach for the second one. Both are quite small, and each one could easily fit in a person's hand. But, again I wouldn't call them dainty with all of their ornate and heavy look-ing features.

I open the second one and it plays the same tune. It's kind of odd, now that I think about it, that they were stored in what I assumed was another jewelry box. I wonder if the larger box was used for something else and Grandma just put the music boxes in it for shipping. I'll probably never know . . . unless Mario has some clues. Definitely questions for Mario, whenever I meet him.

Only one more of Grandma's brown boxes left to open. It's past lunch time but I really want to have all of these boxes opened before I contact my attorney and decide what to do with my jewelry.

Again, the doorbell startles me out of my thoughts and Shadow darts under the chair to hide.

My goodness, this is like Grand Central Station around here.

Chapter 7

Once again a delivery man hands me an envelope and asks me to sign for it. Just like the last guy, he looks past my foyer and asks if I'm in the middle of cleaning or moving.

Why do these delivery men care what I'm doing? For that matter, when was the last time I actually talked to a delivery man about anything other than the weather?

Thanking him for the envelope, I lay it beside the last one and go back to my last box in the living room.

Box number 10 is heavy as I slide it away from the other pile. Opening it, I see why. It's full of cookbooks. Aged and well used ones are stacked next to ones without wear and tear and leftover flour. Definitely all have been used, though. I will cherish these as I know Grandma used them from Venice to the US. I may even try some of her favorite recipes she has marked.

As I eat lunch I will skim through these instead of the diaries to see if anything jumps out at me. I go back to thinking about her words as she lay dying in the hospital. Still, nothing makes a lot of sense. If I remember correctly, she had several warnings and comments for me. Was she really lucid enough to send me warnings? Why warnings? It's not exactly like she lived an exciting or dangerous life. She was a pastry chef, for goodness sake.

Let's see if I can remember what she said.

"They're all yours", could mean she was talking about the jewelry and the music boxes. She would know I was her only heir, so why would she make such a big deal out of telling me this? And, why weren't they in her will?

"It's in the cookbook", could mean there is something in one of these cookbooks that explains the jewelry. I originally thought she was talking about recipes. Now, I'm thinking it's more apt to be something related to the jewelry. But, it could be nothing more than a new recipe. How am I going to know the difference, even if I see it?

"People will try to steal it . . . or them . . . or something", could mean most anything. I can't even really remember exactly what she said. Again, she could have been referring to the jewelry. I can definitely see why someone would want to steal all of it. But first, wouldn't they have to know I have it? And, why didn't anyone try to steal it from her? Or, maybe they did and I didn't know it. No, she would have told me if she had a break-in.

Now, I'm also trying to remember what her attorney told me. I know Mario is to contact me. I certainly hope he does. And, I really hope he has some light to shed on all of this. I know I need to get the jewelry appraised but I need to contact my attorney first to get a good recommendation for an appraiser. And, where on earth am I going to keep all of this? If it's as valuable as it looks, I need to invest in a safe or something.

Shadow reminds me it's way past his lunchtime, so back to the kitchen to fill his food bowl.

Wait . . . what about these envelopes the two odd delivery guys brought to me? Come to think of it, they could have been the same guy or at least brothers. They reminded me of each other. In fact, they also reminded me of someone I've seen before. The way they wore their caps and the way they looked out from underneath their caps certainly make me think of someone else. But who?

No time to worry about that. I'll open these envelopes as soon I as feed my starving Shadow.

Chapter 8

"Shadow, I can't take any more surprises in one day. Can I?" Shadow looks up from his bowl of food and purrs.

Taking a deep breath, I look at the first envelope. The return address says it's from Grandma's attorney, so he must have forgotten to give something to me. Ripping it open, I discover a smaller envelope containing a single sheet of paper. Skimming to the bottom, I see it's from Grandma written about a month before she died.

Talk about shock. It's a good thing I don't have heart issues or I'd be lying on the kitchen floor right now. I should call her attorney and give him an earful. Not sure what good that would do, however, as Grandma was persuasive and probably adamant about what he was to do with this envelope and when he was to mail it to me.

Taking a deep breath, I read it carefully.

Dearest Marta,

I'm writing to you as I know I don't have long to live. I'm 95 . . . almost 96 and I'm tired. I'm sorry to have kept this all from you, but there are reasons why. Mario can fill you in on the details as that story is too long for this letter.

I never wanted anyone to come looking for you. I'm afraid the wrong people want what isn't theirs. People you know. But, there are some good people in North Beach that have helped me keep my secrets. They understand how history contains secrets. Trust them.

Since I'm sure you've opened the boxes I had sent to you and probably have plenty of questions, I'll try to give you some answers. But understanding some of the answers will only create many more questions. Some of these questions can only be answered by Mario and by going to my estate in Italy.

Yes, I have an estate in Italy . . . and a small palace. The estate, located near Conegliano, started out as a small farm that had been in our family for generations, growing grapes for our family and for local use. Then, my mother's land was deeded to me when she died. I was only 17. Since Dad had purchased some adjoining land with more vineyards, and created a partnership with a talented winemaker, our land produced some of the best Italian Prosecco. Dad was savvy and a bit of an entrepreneur. He also purchased a rundown, former palace in Venice and renovated it. Once he sold it to an upscale hotel, he purchased another smaller one, renovated it, and turned that villa into our home.

When I was young, we moved into the villa in Venice part time. Mother used to worry about her land and the vineyards, only I didn't realize it at the time. She always told me the vineyards contained secrets. I didn't understand what she was talking about for a long time. Dad never wanted to talk about anything related to her or her land. Ask Mario to show you around the villa.

In Venice, I discovered my love of baking and trained with a talented pastry chef. His son, Luigi, and I became good friends. Luigi would visit our farm and I would stay with them when my family wasn't in Venice. We knew every inch of Venice, every back alley, every tiny canal, and we knew every inch of the farmland in the foothills. Everything was an adventure to us. More on that later. Mario is Luigi's grandson. You'll like him.

Now, the villa in Venice is yours to do with what you want. It's completely furnished and has a staff that will get it ready for you. I know it wasn't in my will as it is already in your name. My attorney in Italy will handle it now that I'm gone. He knows what to do. Venice is expensive to live in these days. You may want to rent it out or sell it. That's entirely up to you.

As for the land, you share that with the winemaker's grandson. Your name has been on that deed as well since you were 21. I've always signed your name for both properties. Hope you don't mind . . . The rights to the Prosecco brand are shared between the two of you.

What do you think of the jewelry? Pretty spectacular, huh? That is, if you like that style of jewelry. And those music boxes. Technically, it's all yours. Legally, too. I'll explain later.

Find the old book with the map and key to the jewelry and music boxes. Mario can help you. He should be contacting you shortly and you can go to Venice to meet with him and my attorney.

Have to go now. I'm getting tired. I will write more later.

Love, Grandma

That's it. She doesn't write any more. And, she's right. I do have more questions. Loads more questions.

Secrets and legal issues are definitely beyond comprehension. I don't understand the jewelry issue, I don't know who would come looking for me, I don't know whom to trust or how I'll know whom to trust, I don't know about owning a palace and vineyards, I don't know anything . . .

"Shadow, I need answers." Shadow just looks at me and purrs.

"A lot of help, you are."

Maybe the second envelope contains another letter from Grandma. That would definitely be helpful.

Chapter 9

Picking up the second envelope, I see no return address. That's odd. Perhaps her attorney forgot.

Opening this one, I find another smaller envelope inside. Excited that I will learn more about Grandma's life and my inheritance, I rip open that envelope and a small, folded piece of paper floats out.

Unfolding it, the words stare up at me.

Nothing is at it seems. Trust no one. Be careful. They are watching you.

"What the hell?" Dropping the sheet in my lap, I grab the delivery envelope again to make sure there was no return address. Nope. Did Grandma send this one, too? It's definitely not her handwriting. I look at the words again. Yep, I read them correctly. And they still make no sense. No sense at all.

Deciding I need to find out more about these letters, I place a call to Grandma's attorney in Minnesota. He shed light on the first envelope as he did comply with Grandma's wishes and sent it to me on the appointed date. But, he knew nothing of the second one and could not give me any clarification as to what those words meant. He didn't know if Grandma had any enemies and no idea why anyone would send me a letter like that. He also told me when she mentioned her attorney in Italy, he researched him and then contacted him. He assured me he is someone I can trust.

Then, he gave me a couple names of people Grandma visited here in North Beach. They were names I already recognized, but thanked him anyway.

Now, it's time to make some plans, clean up my living room, check my email, organize my dinner party, and put aside Grandma's cookbooks to read. Not sure what I'm looking for, I'll start with the newest ones and work my way through them. Sliding the heavy box of cookbooks closer to the sofa, I decide to start on those tonight.

First, though, I need to call my attorney about the jewelry and then I can move the rest of the boxes to the guest room for storage for now. Folding up both letters and their envelopes, I make my way to my home office at the back of the house. I'll look at these more closely later and start a list of questions for Mario . . . if he ever contacts me.

Filling my attorney in on some of the details, I tell him my grandma left me some jewelry she suggested I have appraised. Since I don't know a lot about the value of jewelry I told him I wanted a trustworthy person. We talked some about her estate, about her property, which is now mine, in Italy and my plans for moving forward with her wishes.

Finishing that conversation, I give the jeweler he suggested a call and make an appointment for tomorrow morning. He was curious but polite. Telling him I recently inherited some interesting jewelry from my grandma, I wanted to know if I should keep it or if it was worth selling. Not really expecting to see someone so quickly, I had better decide what pieces I should take with me. I'm not sure why, but it doesn't seem smart to take it all to him. Not sure I could even carry it all, anyway.

By taking one brooch, one or two rings, a necklace, and one of the music boxes, I'll at least have someplace to start on understanding what I have and what the value is. It's possible I have a bunch of pretty colored stones that are worth about as much as the brown packing box. Somehow, though, I don't think so.

Wrapping up the pieces to take tomorrow, I carefully set those in a large purse. Everything else remains in their boxes and goes into one of the guest rooms with the rest of Grandma's boxes.

Now it's time to eat my dinner, finalize my dinner party to do list, and make a last minute grocery list. Good thing everything else is already done. At least the guest list has already been confirmed. No surprises there.

Chapter 10

What a strange chain of events with Mr. Johnson, the jeweler who appraised my jewelry. Back at home and putting groceries away, I recall the entire bizarre visit.

Mr. Johnson actually gushed as I took each piece out of my purse and laid it on the mat on his counter. That was weird. Then he muttered more to himself than me about the value and quality. I kept asking him what he said. He'd look at me like he had forgotten I was even there.

I thought he was going to faint when I showed him the music box. His eyes lit up, he rubbed his hands together, and I swear he started dancing. He must have asked me five times where I got it. When I told him I inherited all of it, his demeanor changed and he asked me when and where. He really wanted to know more about this than I was willing or ready to tell him.

When I asked if that was important, he replied "I just would like to know." When I didn't respond to him, he asked me another series of questions. "Whom did you inherit these from? Do I know her? Do you have other things? Is she from San Francisco?" Strange.

He then told me he was pretty sure all the pieces I brought to him were antiques. Since I had already figured that, I asked how old. "They could be at least 100 years old or maybe even older," he stated emphatically.

"A hundred years? How on earth would Grandma have pieces that were 100 years old? Maybe they were in the family and passed down from generation to generation. That would make sense. Right?"

He shook his head and said "I don't think so."

"Why not? How do you know?"

"Trust me, I've seen pieces like these and they belong to royalty. Was your grandmother from a royal family?"

"I don't think so. What kind of royalty?"

"I'm talking kings and queens."

I needed time to think about this. Pointing to the music box, which was still sitting by his right hand, I asked him what he thought of that.

"Definitely worth several hundred thousand dollars. I would know more after some research. Would you like to leave it here?" He almost caressed it as he talked.

"Several hundred thousand," I managed to squeak out. Not wanting to sound greedy, I hesitantly asked, "And the rest of the jewelry?"

"I'd have to do a little research on that as well, but initially I'd say the collection you brought in could be worth around several hundred thousand, especially if it's as old as I think it is. If not, it would still be valued at around somewhere close to that." Again, he told me I could leave it with him. This time his suggestion was more of a command. I was getting a little uncomfortable with his obsession with my music box.

I nodded. Since I couldn't quite comprehend everything Mr. Johnson told me, I said I would be taking everything home with me.

He seemed genuinely disappointed. "If you're sure. Otherwise, I could keep it for you. It's not a problem for me to do that."

When I told him again I would take it, he sighed. "I'll write up an appraisal sheet for your insurance company. You do have insurance on these, don't you? Where are you going to keep them? Any time you want me to look at them some more, you can drop them off here. We could make another appointment."

I couldn't imagine what Mr. Johnson would say if I told him this was only a very small portion of the collection Grandma left to me.

Wrapped carefully in soft gray cloths, Mr. Johnson handed each piece to me. "I'll give you that appraisal sheet if you can wait a couple of minutes. Keep in mind it's a preliminary appraisal. I will give a range and will narrow it down once I do some research. This will suffice for your insurance company for now."

Once the pieces were placed back in my purse, I noticed Mr. Johnson's assistant staring at me. If I wasn't in a reliable jeweler's shop, this guy would give me the creeps. Smiling at him, I asked how his day had been going.

He shrugged and looked down. I wondered how long he'd been standing there and if he saw my jewelry.

"You have a great job, looking at all these fine pieces every day," I tried to engage him in conversation. Maybe he'd stop staring.

Finally, Mr. Johnson came back with the appraisals. He addressed his assistant, "Pete, please finalize the bill of sale for our two o'clock client. She called to tell me she's coming early." Pete nodded and left the room. I hated to tell Mr. Johnson I didn't like Pete staring at me. Perhaps he was just mesmerized by the music box.

Still, he was creepy.

The whole appointment was puzzling.

Chapter 11

Now I have a little bit of time to look through a few cookbooks while I eat lunch and then I really must get ready for my party. I'll continue looking through the newest ones first and work my way back to her older ones.

I love looking through cookbooks but I have no idea what I should be looking for. I only have Grandma's dying words stuck in my mind that something is in one of these. So far, nothing looks like a secret recipe or any type of code I could use to figure out what she meant. There are a lot of cookbooks to look through. While there are many awesome sounding recipes, some with notes Grandma wrote beside them and some with lines drawn through them, I'm beginning to wonder if she really was just mumbling about something important being in one of these.

I'm sure not.

Looking at the stacks surrounding me, I realize I don't have room to display all of them in my kitchen. For now, I'll keep them on bookshelves in my office and figure out a way to keep a few in the kitchen so I'll have Grandma looking over my shoulder as I bake. Taking the ones I looked at to my office bookshelves, I make two piles of the remaining cookbooks. One pile contains smaller, older looking books . . . some even look like they may be handwritten. Sure hope they're in English. The other pile has ones that look old but not as worn.

Deciding to finish these much later while I eat dinner, I stack them on the kitchen counter just as the doorbell rings.

Mr. Johnson's assistant, Pete, is at my door. "You forgot your appraisal sheet."

Looking at him and knowing full well I didn't I tell him, "Oh. Thanks. I thought I put it in my purse."

"Nope." Apparently Pete is a man of few words. This constant staring is getting to me.

Being slightly uncomfortable that Pete knows where I live, "Thanks. Next time you can call me and I'll come get it. Be sure to tell Mr. Johnson thank you as well."

Pete turns to leave and looks back at me with that creepy stare, "If you need any help selling those or if you find more of them, let me know. I know people who like that type of thing."

Now I'm really uncomfortable. Wanting him to leave as quickly as possible, once again I tell Pete, "Thanks."

Shutting the door firmly and making sure all the locks are locked, I turn to see Shadow peering out from around the corner . . . all fluffed up, looking like he does when something spooks him. "So, you don't like him, either? And, you're the best judge of character I know. What is it about him? I'm going to call Mr. Johnson right now and tell him I really don't want Pete coming to my house anymore."

Shadow, now back to normal size, just purrs.

Chapter 12

Putting the phone down, I turn to Shadow. "You really know people, don't you? It's too bad you didn't attack him. Do you know what Mr. Johnson told me? Of course you don't."

Shadow sits down and proceeds to wash his ears. I continue on as if he cares what I'm saying . . .

"He told me Pete walked off the job and took several appraisal sheets with him while Mr. Johnson was at lunch. Mr. Johnson seemed distracted and hurried, like he really didn't want to talk to me. He kept asking if there was anything else I needed. I told him Pete was here with a copy of my appraisal sheet and he was surprised. When I asked him if he let the police know about the stolen appraisal sheets, he nervously stuttered and said he had to go. Then he abruptly hung up.

"You know what, Shadow? I really don't like Pete. I am going to call the police and just ask what I should do about my appraisal sheet being taken and about Pete being here. They may tell me it's nothing and then I'll be relieved."

I called. After a few questions, I was transferred to another person. A few more questions and then she told me they were sending two detectives to my house. Detectives? Who would have thought appraisal sheets were so valuable?

Sure enough, two detectives show up at my house only minutes later. Agents Mark Smith and Lynne Greystone introduce themselves, asking me to call them Mark and Lynne. Efficient, in control, and yet pleasant they take out notepads as we sit it my living room. They want to hear what I know about Pete and the appraisal sheets.

I start my story with the jewelry shop, tell them Pete came to my house, and finish with my phone call to Mr. Johnson. My detailed description of Pete matches ones they already had. They can obtain surveillance camera video from the shop along with his fingerprints, as I am informed they're sure this is the person they are looking for in connection with several other jewelry thefts.

I'm still confused about all of this. More like astonished, really. Appraisal sheets warrant this much detective work?

Asking me what Pete knows about my business at the jewelers, I tell them I was having some jewelry appraised. When asked if it is valuable, I tell them it has not only sentimental value to me because of Grandma, but that the jeweler valued it at several hundred thousand.

Raising their eyebrows and looking at me, Agent Mark asks if he heard me correctly. Removing the appraisal from my purse and showing it to them, they ask where I'm keeping the jewelry.

"For now, it's safe." I tell them. "But, I want to move it somewhere safer."

Realizing that made no sense, I tell them it's a long story that even I don't quite understand yet. Now I've really confused them. Looking at each other, Agent Mark leans back and says, "We have time."

Starting at the beginning, I give them a brief version from Grandma's dying words, unpacking the jewelry and the music boxes, and going to Mr. Johnson's for an appraisal. When they ask if they could see one or two pieces, I excuse myself and retrieve a necklace and a music box.

Stunned, they look at both pieces, then at each other, and then back at me.

"I've seen this music box before," Agent Lynne says. "I know I've seen it."

"I agree with you," Agent Mark concurs. "May we handle it and open it?" He looks at me.

"Sure."

"Do you know where your grandma acquired this?"

"Not at all. I thought I knew everything about Grandma, but this came as a total surprise to me. Especially after I learned the value of it."

Opening the box, its tune softly filled the living room. Agent Lynne looks at her partner and asks, "It's the same tune, isn't it?"

Once again I'm confused. "Same as what?"

"We may have some information about another music box that would fit with the description of yours. But, it's important we know how and where your grandma acquired this and how long she's had it in her possession."

"I wish I knew any of that," I tell them. "I honestly wish I knew."

Chapter 13

Inspecting my music box more carefully, Agent Lynne writes some notes about markings, size, and the tune it plays. Agent Mark makes a couple of phone calls and comes back to visit with Agent Lynne. The two of them whisper to each other, nodding their heads, finally looking up at me.

"We think, based on the description of another music box like this one, they were part of a royal collection from the early 1600s. We won't know for absolute certain until we have our art expert examine both of them. Take a look at this photo on my phone that I just had emailed to me. They look alike. But, we're not jewelry experts at all."

Looking at the email, I'm getting more confused by the minute. "What? I don't understand any of this. They do look alike. But, the 1600s? Why wouldn't Grandma tell me she had something this valuable and this old? And, where did that one come from? Was Pete involved in appraising that one, too?"

"Marta, we have a lot more investigation to do on this. We don't know everything there is to know yet. The photo of this one was taken before it was stolen from a businessman who lives here in San Francisco. We've called in an investigator of stolen art to help figure out what is going on and to help recover the stolen music box. His name is Clark and he works regularly with agencies that need his art expertise."

Nodding like I understood, "You don't think these are the same piece, do you? My grandma certainly wouldn't have stolen property."

They reassured me, "Not at all. Clark, the investigator, said there was a royal collection of music boxes like this one dating back to the 1600s. Valuable in their own way and unique, sort of like Faberge eggs. He thinks originally there were 10 of these made for some royal family in Venice, Italy or possibly Hungary."

At this revelation, my ears perked up. "Venice?"

"Yes, Venice. Why do you ask?"

"My grandmother was born somewhere in that area and worked and lived in Venice before coming to the United States."

Upon hearing this, both detectives look at each other and back to me. It appears more information is coming my way. "Did she live in Venice recently?"

"Not at all. She came to the US shortly after World War II, but she has returned to visit there a few times since. Why?"

"According to Clark, the music boxes were probably lost during World War I or before. Most figured they had been destroyed."

"How do you know so much about these music boxes?" I asked. "After all, I would imagine this type of theft is not in your normal work days."

Agent Mark filled me in. "We were assigned the case of the stolen one several months ago. The owner in North Beach was killed and this was the only thing missing from his house. It started out as a robbery turned homicide. Now, things are getting confusing."

"North Beach? Who was it?"

"The man's name was Giovanni and he owned a butcher shop. Why?"

"I know him. Or, at least my grandma knew him and I met him several times. I've even bought meat from his shop. He's dead? Oh my goodness. What happened to the music box? Did you find out who killed him? Why would someone kill for a music box?

35

Oh right, it's valuable. Did he have any other valuable things in his house?"

I can't seem to stop asking questions.

"Slow down. At this point, it's still an open investigation. Learning more about these music boxes is helpful. We'll let Clark know about yours and he can interview you. That way you can keep it safe. Speaking of that . . . you really need to invest in a safe or go to the bank to a safe deposit box. Especially now that Pete knows you have it. We still need to talk to him." Agent Mark made some more notes as he stood up.

"Wait a minute." Now seemed like as good a time as any to let them know about the other one. "I have more."

"More what?" they asked in unison.

"Wait here, please." I left the living room to bring out the second music box.

Chapter 14

Carefully setting it on the coffee table beside the first one, it was easy to see how they could belong to a set. They complimented each other in style, yet each had its own distinctive look. One was bolder, with larger gemstones. The other was slightly daintier, with more filigree work woven into the design.

Looking at them sitting side by side, Agent Mark asked, "Do you have any more?"

Not even thinking the rest of the jewelry would be connected, I said, "No, these are the only two I have." The detectives hadn't mentioned anything about the necklace I originally brought out and I wasn't really concentrating on that.

"Okay . . . you really need to keep these safe. Is your home alarm system a good one? I need to make a couple of calls. We're going to make sure there are regular police patrols past your house, just to discourage Pete and his friends from making an unscheduled visit. Once you visit with Clark, you can look into a home safe."

Now I'm getting a little more concerned. Pete really gives me the creeps and I told that to the detectives. They assured me there would be enough police presence and plain clothes police in the neighborhood for the next several weeks. That would give me time to either purchase a quality safe or to find a safe place for these.

"I think we're finished for now," as Agents Mark and Lynne stood up to leave. "We can't stress enough how you need to protect these items. And, we don't even really know much about art! It's amazing what some people will do, though, to steal something they want or something they can sell."

Tentatively, I asked "Do you really think Pete or his friends are involved? Do you think he would come back to see if he could steal it?"

"We can't say for sure. But guys like Pete see only the dollar signs. Just be careful."

After thanking them and locking the door behind them, I realized I spent most of the afternoon talking to the detectives. Problem is . . . I still don't know any more about Grandma's music boxes, where they came from, or why she had them. In fact, none of my questions have been answered.

I guess it's time to do some research about these and hope Mario contacts me so I can ask him about the music boxes.

First, though, it's time to fix dinner, sit down with a glass of wine, and read some more cookbooks.

Chapter 15

Whew! Yesterday was a blur.

First, the visit to Mr. Johnson, the jeweler, and his creepy assistant, Pete, who wasn't really his assistant, then discussing the whole thing with the SFPD detectives, doing some preliminary research on the music boxes, and finishing my night with clues and questions from Grandma's cookbooks.

"Shadow, what is going on?" Shadow rolls over to have his belly rubbed as I walk past him on the way to the kitchen to make coffee.

Since tonight is my dinner party and I have some new clients coming, I can waste no time today trying to figure out anything more about anything. I must concentrate on cooking and getting ready for the party. If I'm organized, maybe I'll have some time to do a little more Internet searching about missing music boxes from the 1600s and more time to decipher Grandma's notes in her cookbooks. It's all a lot more time consuming than I thought.

Grabbing some coffee while working on the dessert for tonight, I'm interrupted by the phone. Answering it on the third ring, no one is there. Heavens . . . have a little patience, caller. My caller ID just says 'private', so that's not a lot of help.

The morning passes quickly and I'm almost completely organized for tonight. Things that need to go in the oven are prepped and ready. Everything else is in its final stages and just need to be taken care of at the last minute. My phone rings for the third time. Phone call number two was from the same private number . . . and no one was there, either.

This time, one of my clients, Mrs. Moreno, calls to apologize for a last minute addition to my guest list. She's such a sweetheart that I couldn't get upset with her for adding one more person at this late hour. She tells me her nephew will be accompanying her. "He's so interesting and such a nice man, I think you'll enjoy him. He travels a bunch and recently returned from Europe and I just had to bring him. I really hope you don't mind."

Assuring her it was okay with me, inwardly I groan. Is she trying to set us up? That would be just like her. I really don't have time to start dating a man I've never met, especially right now. But, I'll find a way to fit him in and hopefully he won't be trying to wrangle a date with me.

Time for a late lunch as I look over the last two cookbooks again. Up until I read those, nothing seemed like anything more than just recipes with Grandma's helpful notes in the margins. But, these last two seem to be the oldest cookbooks. They are written in Italian and then translated into English. I'm not sure they were ever formal cookbooks, but more like ones somebody put together to record and keep some favorite recipes.

Unless you knew what you were looking for, I'm not sure her notes would indicate anything other than where to find special ingredients. But, the more I think about what she had written, the more I think those notes go with one or more of her maps. Anyway, she keeps mentioning maps in her cookbook. That's odd unless they really do go together. I just need to figure out how and which ones. And, I don't even know if it all means something related to the jewelry or the music boxes.

Which brings me to my research on the music boxes . . .

The detectives were right. It seems there was a series of 10 different, small music boxes. All valuable with gemstones and jewels attached in 18 karat gold. And, they do have some Venetian history associated with them. The rest gets fuzzy . . . the French, Austrian, Popes, the Turkish Empire, and more all ruled Venice at one time and left their influence on art and history.

I couldn't find who made these boxes or why; only that they once existed and then vanished. It appears they vanished more than once. But, they always seemed to surface somewhere in Italy. During World War I, they vanished for the final time. There is all sorts of speculation about them and what happened to them.

I'm so confused about the whole story. Maybe it's just that . . . a story. Yet, they're real. And, they're valuable.

And, I haven't even started to research the jewelry.

Chapter 16

Guests are arriving, mingling, and enjoying champagne . . . and Shadow is in hiding. Just as I think Mrs. Moreno and her nephew aren't coming at all, the doorbell rings and someone greets them for me. Apologizing for coming at the last minute and for being late, Mrs. Moreno introduces me to her nephew, Clark. Tall, dark, and handsome come to mind. With an air around him that says he's in control, Clark flashes a 100 watt smile at me. Whoa.

It runs through my mind that until this week I didn't even know anyone named Clark and now I've heard that name twice. Strange.

We don't really have time to chat as I need to get everyone seated so I can serve the first course. During one of my trips to the kitchen, Clark helps clear some plates and tells me he would like to visit with me sometime after dinner. Yep, he wants a date . . . Smiling, I tell him I would love to chat but I'm pretty busy right now.

Throughout the evening everyone appears to be having a good time, if you can judge by the noise level. We've eaten and enjoyed our silky squash soup, butter lettuce salad with crispy prosciutto, and entrée of bacon wrapped pork tenderloin with green beans and polenta. Dessert, tiny cream puffs filled with chocolate cream, was a hit and many are lingering over coffee or brandy.

Mrs. Moreno and Clark approach me to thank me and tell me goodbye.

"I'm sorry I haven't had time to get back to you and chat," I tell Clark.

"No worries. But, Agent Mark Smith suggested I talk to you. We should set a time that works for you."

I'm sure the color drained from my face. "Are you the Clark the detectives were talking about? The one who is working with the SFPD about some stolen art?"

Looking around, Clark lowers his voice, "Well, as of today it's more than the SFPD. The FBI and Interpol are also involved. We really need to talk. Soon. You'll probably have more investigators here in the next couple of days. You do have a good alarm system, right?"

Nodding my head, I seem to have forgotten how to speak.

"Good. Why don't we set a time for tomorrow? I can come here around ten o'clock if that works for you. We need to get a good start on this."

"Okay." I'm breathless.

Chapter 17

Shrill screeching, followed by a series of high pitched, piercing beeps jolts me out of bed. In the dark, I can barely make out Shadow as he dives under the bed. I might be fully awake, but I'm not comprehending anything at the moment. Then it hits me. That's my security alarm.

And, it's not stopping.

Grabbing my phone to punch in 911, my alarm company calls. It's a good thing the detectives took care of informing SFPD about my situation. My alarm dispatcher asked very few questions, telling me police were already in my neighborhood and would call me before they came to my door.

Now, to stop that noise so I can hear myself think.

My phone rings again and I answer it without looking at the caller ID, thinking it's the police. It's not.

"You were lucky this time. Next time, maybe not." The husky, muted voice spits out at me and hangs up.

Scared out of my wits for the second time this night, I look around at windows, my half lit living room, and dark corners of my house. When my phone rings again, I check the screen and see the call is from the police.

Two officers sit in my kitchen and take notes while I fill them in on my phone call from husky voice guy. One officer calls Agent Mark, who says he's on his way over.

Once again, I explain the events . . . my alarm going off, the call from husky voice guy, and finally the call from the police. Of course they want to take my phone to see if they can get anything off of it. I can tell they're doubtful but still need to check it out.

The two police officers were only two blocks away, having just driven past my house minutes before my alarm went off. Either someone was watching them leave or that person got lucky. They don't believe in luck.

When I relate the events of last night's party to Agent Mark, he's glad that I will be meeting with Clark sooner than later. He wasn't yet aware of the FBI and Interpol being involved but is glad to hear that.

Hesitating, I can tell he has more to tell me. "There was another murder and robbery. For some reason, these music boxes are surfacing now and creating quite the activity. And, it's not good activity."

Asking him, "Was it here in San Francisco? Was it anybody I knew?"

He tells me, "No. This time it was a man in San Diego. His daughter went to check on him because he missed their regular Friday night dinner and she found him. His throat was slit. As far as she can tell, the only thing missing is a small music box she used to listen to as a little girl. The house wasn't even tossed . . ."

Getting the feeling he isn't telling me the whole story, I ask, "What? What aren't you telling me?"

"Marta, this music box was given to him by his grandfather."

"Okay."

"His grandfather came from northern Italy, and supposedly worked for some well-connected people. Some could have been royalty, according to his stories. The daughter wasn't exactly sure."

My brain is working overtime and Agent Mark can sense that. "Marta, don't read any more into this until after you talk to Clark. We don't know what this means."

"Don't you see? They have to be connected. My grandmother has to be connected to him somehow. Should I talk to his daughter? Maybe I need to read Grandma's diaries more carefully. I can go get them now."

"Slow down. Didn't you say Clark was coming here at ten o'clock? That's only three hours from now. Take a deep breath. Talk to him first and then we'll all figure out a plan."

Agreeing that's best, I show the officers and Agent Mark to the door and reset the alarm. Knowing I won't get any more sleep, I'll sit down with Grandma's cookbooks and journals after a quick shower.

"Maybe I should bring out the box of maps, too." I tell Shadow, who has now reappeared and is giving himself a bath.

Chapter 18

Surrounded by boxes, cookbooks, and old maps, I'm taking notes and marking pages as the doorbell rings. Assuming it's Clark, I open the door, ready to pick his brain so I can formulate a plan.

It's not Clark. Once more a delivery guy shoves a hand held computer at me and tells me to sign for yet another envelope. I really need to be more careful about opening this door. This guy is not quite as sullen and unfriendly as the last ones, and at least he didn't want to ask about my stuff.

Hoping this is another letter from Grandma, I open the delivery envelope only to find a cream colored envelope embossed with the initial M. Hmm. Looks like an invitation. Carefully opening that one, I see two pieces of paper. It's not an invitation . . . well not exactly.

Dearest Marta,

First of all, condolences on losing your grandmother. She was such a special person to me.

You don't know me, but I knew your grandmother. My grandfather was Luigi, a good friend of your grandmother. I wish you could have met him.

Your grandmother's attorney has contacted me with the details in her will. He has also given me your contact information per her wishes.

You may or may not know about some special items your grandmother had. There are many things we need to discuss, including these items. If you have already discovered them, you probably have many questions. Please don't let anyone talk you into selling them. And, please trust no one when referring to these items.

If you are totally confused, I apologize.

If you have already found a great deal of jewelry and some music boxes, then you will understand what I'm talking about.

We need to meet as soon as possible. My family's private jet will be in San Francisco tomorrow to pick you up and bring you to Venice. Again, I apologize for the short notice but it can't be helped. You can stay with my family or at your own residence in Venice. I took the liberty of asking the staff to get it ready for you.

Please tell as few people as possible where you are going. I know that sounds clandestine, but there are some recent events that have taken place causing me to be extra careful. Please bring several of the jewelry pieces and your music boxes with you when you come. A limo will arrive at your home at six o'clock tomorrow evening to pick you up. You can trust the driver to help you with everything you need to bring.

The details of your flight are on a separate sheet. You should be prepared to be in Italy for at least two to three weeks. We may not get everything done in that timeframe, but you can return at a later date to complete any unfinished business.

There is just one last thing that has come to my attention. An art investigator, Clark Moreno, may be able to contact you before you leave. He is the only one

I would trust with any of this information. Otherwise, trust no one else.

I will meet you at the airport in Venice.

Ciao,
Mario

Chapter 19

Reading the letter once more to make sure I'm really leaving tomorrow, I'm a little relieved and a whole lot more confused.

"Well, Shadow, you're going to have to stay with Julie again. Sorry about that, but I know you like her. She gives you treats whenever you want them."

When the doorbell rings for the second time this morning, I glance outside before opening it. Clark is standing on the doorstep with a laptop computer, camera, and some large brown envelopes.

"You won't believe my morning," I start to tell him as he simultaneously says, "It's been quite a whirlwind the last couple of days."

Gesturing for him to come in and put everything on the dining room table, "You go first."

"Let me fill you in on a little of what I do before I get into the specifics of the music boxes. I grew up here in North Beach, my grandpa was a chef here, I always loved art and puzzles, I'm a Marine who joined a special task force with the FBI, then formed my own business, and now I use everything I know to catch thieves who steal high end art. Throw in a few murders and I call in the regular cops and sometimes the FBI."

Nodding, I'm beginning to realize more than I want.

Continuing on, "Usually thieves go after a piece because a collector wants it and can't get in the legal way. Sometimes, they steal for the money they make selling it on the black market. Sometimes we catch the bad guys. Sometimes we don't. Usually there aren't this many murders associated with a piece of stolen art. But then, this is quite the collection.

"Now I need to know your story, what you have, where you got it, and everything else you can possibly think of. Oh, I forgot to tell you . . . I met your grandmother. She was a good friend of my grandpa and would visit him when she came here."

Realizing things are getting more connected all the time, I take a deep breath and fill Clark in on the details. All the details, starting with Grandma in the hospital and ending with Mario's letter.

While I'm talking, Clark is taking some notes and scratching Shadow's chin. Shadow is purring.

Finishing my whole tale, I ask if he wants to see everything Grandma left to me. Since what I consider to be relevant cookbooks, maps, and journals have all been moved back to the living room, I let him start looking through those as I bring out the jewelry box and the music boxes.

"You have quite the collection. I know I've seen some of it before," as he's looking at my jewelry.

"Really? Where?"

"I will check some of my notes to be sure. Let me get my laptop going and I can tell you more. In the meantime, do you have any idea how long your grandma had all of these items?"

"Not at all. In fact, I didn't even know she had any of this. We were so close and yet now I'm wondering if I really knew her at all. After late reading, I finally found some notes in one of the cookbooks that led me to a map. When I finally found the map, I found notes on it saying to cross reference with Luigi's map and a book. She doesn't say which book. At least Grandma was thorough and made notes, but Luigi is dead and I have no idea where his map is. Wait a minute. Maybe Mario has them and that's why he wanted me to bring everything. By everything, I assumed he meant the jewelry and the music boxes. But, maybe I need to bring the old cookbooks and maps as well. It's all so confusing."

Clark, who by this time has his laptop up and running, is looking at some photos of jewelry. "See these pieces? They look just like yours. And, you know what? They are missing. They've been missing since the 1940s. Apparently, they were owned by some descendants of some royalty . . . not sure where from but indications lead to Austria. The history is kind of fuzzy after that.

"Anyway, they were stolen as Italy was in turmoil just before or during World War I. Again, speculation . . . but it's rumored that enemy troops ransacked a castle or a palace and stole jewelry, artwork, and anything else that looked valuable. Turns out the art was sold and recently recovered. It's now back where it belongs in a museum in Vienna. Some of the crystal and the statues were never recovered though.

"Here's where it gets interesting. There were also 10 ornate, small music boxes. Each one was different but all were inlaid with jewels and 18 karat gold. Four were recovered when someone got careless and tried to sell them to an undercover agent. This was about five years ago.

"Now, we know two were recently stolen and tied to murders in each case. And, we know you have two more of them. But, who knows you have them?"

"I did have one of them appraised by a supposed reliable jeweler here in San Francisco. His assistant wasn't so reliable and in fact came to my house with a tall tale of giving me my appraisal. So, he knows I have one and he knows where I live. He doesn't know I have two of them, however.

"The police and two detectives were here interviewing me about him. They know I have two of the music boxes and they gave me your name as someone I can trust."

"Ahh, that's why I saw both police presence and unmarked cars in the area. Makes sense now."

"So, what's my next step? Other than getting on a private plane to Italy tomorrow, that is."

"You need to go to Venice and take the old cookbooks, the old maps, the music boxes, a few pieces of the jewelry, and photos of the rest of the jewelry with you. I want to take some of the jewelry and really look into it. I also want to find out how your grandma happened to have this spectacular collection. It appears to be old and genuine. It also reminds me of a bracelet my grandpa had . . . but I'm just not sure. I need to investigate some more. I'll also do more research on the music boxes."

When I looked at Clark like he was talking crazy . . . he laughed at me.

"Don't worry about me taking your jewelry. You can leave it with your attorney, the police, the FBI, or whoever. I just need access to it from time to time. And, I don't want you to leave it here."

"Good idea not to leave it here. But, are the police going to continue to watch my house while I'm gone for two weeks?"

"Let's call Agent Mark and figure out the best strategy while you're gone."

Chapter 20

Somewhere over Canada and before I fall asleep it hits me. I have no idea what I'm doing, I have no idea what I'm hoping to find out in Italy, and I have no idea if life, as I used to know it, will ever be the same.

"What did you get yourself into, Grandma? Why didn't you tell me?" Muttering to myself I honestly hope the plan Detectives Mark and Lynne and Clark put into place works. At least one part of this mess will see some resolution.

Anyone watching my house will think I'm gone. What they won't know is that Clark is staying there with Shadow and my jewelry. They also won't know about the new security cameras watching the entire block and my new state-of-the-art safe installed in my guest room closet. I still don't know how they got all that finished in the 18 hours before I left. To the average person, the delivery trucks bringing flowers and new furniture looked like any other deliveries in the neighborhood. Only, they weren't flowers or any new furniture.

I drift off to sleep.

Gently shaking my shoulder the flight attendant informs me we will be landing at the Venice airport in about 30 minutes.

Whew . . . guess I slept right through our refueling stop. Time to freshen up.

As we start our descent, the Alps give way to the rolling plains of the Veneto and then I get a quick glimpse of the lagoon and the iconic tower in the distance. Excited to be back in a city I love, I experience a moment of sadness that Grandma's not with me as we planned to do some day in the near future.

Handing me an envelope, the flight attendant tells me we'll be on the ground in a couple of minutes and that I will find instructions inside.

Marta,

I wish I could meet you at the airport, but I had an issue that needed to be dealt with before you arrived. Our driver, Emilio, will pick you up inside the terminal. Your luggage will be transferred to his water taxi, so don't worry about a thing. He will bring you to our villa. You can then decide where you want to stay while you are here.

I can't wait to meet you.
Ciao,
Mario

Darn it, I was hoping Mario would meet me here at the airport.

Once inside the terminal a handsome, older man with my name on a sign looks at me. Dressed in all black, smiling broadly, he could pass for a chauffeur or a businessman. Hard to tell.

"Buongiorno. I'm Emilio. Benvenuti in Italia. Your luggage will be loaded and then we will leave."

"Grazie." I then try to tell him in Italian that my Italian is rusty as he immediately switches to perfect English.

Producing a bottle and a flute he offers, "Could I pour you a glass of Prosecco while we wait? It's never too early for Prosecco. You can celebrate your return visit to our city." Emilio is gracious, polite, and has a sparkle in his eye. Figuring him to be somewhere in his seventies, I immediately like his easy going nature. And then something else about him strikes me . . .

He's watching everything without appearing to be doing so. His smile never leaves his face and he keeps his eyes on me, but I'm sure he could tell me what everyone in this small terminal is wearing, what their luggage looks like, and where they're going. I'm used to paying close attention to people and places so it's not unusual for me to notice subtleties, but he is a very focused man.

As he turns to speak to the man brining in my luggage is when I catch a glimpse of what appears to be a shoulder holster. Is he carrying a weapon?

Chapter 21

Engaging Emilio in conversation is easy and I like hearing about his Venice. Our water taxi ride is smooth this time of the morning. I love seeing the sun come up across the lagoon and grab my camera for some incredible shots.

Steering the conversation toward Mario, "I've never met him nor even talked to him. Apparently, my grandma knew him as she and his grandfather were good friends."

"Ahh, yes. Your grandmother was special."

It certainly appears my grandma knew a lot of people . . . a lot more than I ever imagined.

Continuing, "Mario's grandfather, Luigi, and your grandma, Lydia, were inseparable when they were growing up and later when they found . . ." Pausing he made gesture with his hand, "certain things."

"I don't really understand all they did and am hoping Mario can fill me in on details of Grandma's life that I don't know anything about. I thought I was so on top of knowing everything about her." Tears begin to fill my eyes.

"Don't cry. Memories come in all shapes. You will have a great time with Mario and you will learn about all the good your grandma did."

That appeared to be all Emilio was going to say as he continued on with his colorful travelogue of the islands and buildings we were passing. Once in the Grand Canal, Emilio slowed the taxi to the required speed. Asking me if I knew which one was mine, I shook my head.

"There. Look at the one on the right with the ornate iron railings. Look past is and down that smaller canal. You can just see the one with a double arch doorway. That's yours. You are fairly close to Mario's. I'll show you the shortcut once we dock."

Idling up to the start of another smaller canal, we dock and another man ties up our boat. Emilio greets him, "Hey, good timing. I'll take Marta's luggage to Palazzo Mario. Please take care of the boat for me and I'll see you later. Thanks."

My luggage is loaded onto a wheeled cart and off we go, Emilio and me. I feel like I should at least help but Emilio tells me no. Down one narrow street, around a corner into an even narrower alley, and over two bridges, we arrive at wider street. Away from the hustle and bustle of tourists, Emilio leads me around one more corner. This is what I love about Venice. I have no idea where I started and where I'm going . . . and somehow I'll be able to find my way back to where I began.

A grand doorway appears on our right, tucked in amongst the buildings. "We're here", announces Emilio. He doesn't even look like he's been working.

I look up. Like most villas and residences in Venice, the doorways, some simple and some grand, are tucked a little off the alley or street and open into a first floor with either worn steps or grand staircases. The living areas are up one flight of stairs, with additional living spaces, bedrooms, and such at least another flight up. This door is magnificent with its carved wood and its lion head door knocker.

Ringing the doorbell, we are greeted by a robust, impossibly handsome man about my age. Over six feet tall, with graying hair at his temples, he possesses a smile that could light up any room. Kissing me on both cheeks, "You're here at last. It's so good to finally meet you. How was the flight? You must be exhausted."

Trying to nod, speak, and take it all in is impossible so I just smile at him.

"Oh my goodness . . . my manners. Welcome to Palace Mario. I'm Mario. I was so excited to finally meet you that I forgot all about being polite. Now, let's start over, shall we?

"Welcome to our home. I live here with my wife, who is currently in Milan for a photo shoot. We are honored to have you as a guest here, especially since I knew your grandmother. And, especially since she and my grandfather were such good friends. Now, let me show you to a room where you can freshen up. You can decide later where you want to stay. We'll have coffee and pastries on the back balcony. If I know Emilio, you've already had Prosecco!"

Smiling and nodding, I'm trying to keep up. Mario has been talking non-stop since I arrived.

Chapter 22

Walking out onto a terrace overlooking a peaceful canal, I think of Grandma and picture her as a little girl growing up here. What fun it must have been to explore all these back canals and alleys. I wonder if I'll get to see the bakery where she first learned to be a pastry chef. There are so many things I want, no need, to see. And, so much to learn.

Smiling as Mario joins me, I tell him my Italian is not good.

"No worries. Everyone in our house speaks English quite well. You can work on your Italian later. Now, let's catch up and then we can decide how to approach what I know and what you know. Okay?"

"Certainly. I'm confused, excited, and amazed all at the same time. I really want to know the whole story about my grandma."

"I understand. First, let me give you a little history of our two families."

Mario started the tale with my grandma meeting his grandpa, Luigi, at Luigi's dad's bakery and how they became great friends as well as respected pastry chefs in their own right. "The kitchen staff and other bakers loved telling them tales about war treasures, pirates, stolen jewels, bad guys, good guys, and who knows what else. Since they both had imaginations, they wrote everything down and thought one day they would each write a book about these stories. They had no idea if the stories were true or not . . . until they heard some of the same things from other people in the area.

"That's when they started thinking some of these might be real. And, they became excited over the prospect of finding lost treasures."

Nodding, I take a notepad out of my bag to take notes as I want to remember all of this.

"I have Grandpa's journals, few that they are, and I assume you have your grandma's journals as well?"

"Yes, I do. Some are in Italian and some have been written in both Italian and English. But, I wasn't able to gain any clues or anything from them. Perhaps I wasn't looking for the right things. In fact, I have no idea what I should be looking for in them."

"I'll continue and that may help you.

"Grandpa and Lydia apparently kept hearing the same stories about different treasures and about a secret escape system in the foothills. Keep in mind, they were pre-teenagers with a sense of adventure. They figured these were worth exploring."

"Is that why Grandma and Luigi would go to her farm and vineyards?"

"For the most part, yes. Staying at Lydia's parents' farm and vineyards, they would explore that area like they explored around Venice. They kept good notes, maps of the area, and cross referenced everything they found. They had no idea what exactly they were looking for, but figured they'd know it when they stumbled across it.

"And, one time they did stumble across more than they had bargained for."

Chapter 23

Dropping my pen and sitting up straighter, "Now you have my attention."

"Did you bring any cookbooks and maps with you?"

"Yes, I brought the three oldest cookbooks. Those seemed to be the only ones with writing that wasn't strictly related to recipes. I also brought one book of maps where Grandma had drawings and writings that seemed to reference those cookbooks. I figured those would be a good start."

"Great. They probably match the few ones I have from Grandpa, but there could be more information in yours. We'll look over both sets later."

Nodding, my phone interrupts our conversation. Looking at the screen, I see it's from Clark. Taking the call, he's probably wondering if I arrived safely. Not exactly . . .

Mario returns to the terrace just as I'm finishing up my call with Clark. I relate the conversation to Mario, "It seems there was an attempted break in at one of my neighbors last night. The new security cameras caught the burglar in the act and the police arrested him just as he was wandering around their home. He kept mumbling something to them about having the wrong address.

Clark will get more information to me when the police are finished questioning him."

"Do you believe it's connected to your house and your newly acquired pieces?"

"I certainly do. And, it's all because I went to the jeweler for an appraisal. I swear that man or assistant or whatever he was, Pete, is involved in more than just trying to steal my jewels."

"I agree. Let's continue on and maybe we can shed some light on all of this."

"Okay . . . please tell me what they stumbled onto . . ."

"First of all, let me give you a little geography of the area. Hills, hills, and more hills make their way into the steep foothills of the Dolomites. It's rocky, uneven terrain with limestone, sandstone, and clay soils that are great for growing grapes but harder than hard to make your way up and down the slopes. And, it's a great place to hide. There are old caves and rocky ledges. You can imagine how much fun it would have been for them to explore as kids. Especially, kids with vivid imaginations.

"Later, when they had what they thought of as secret information, those same hills provided clues to the area's history. You see, there were supposed caves that were used to hide people and valuables. No one ever found anything remotely like these, however. Grandpa told me that didn't prevent them from looking for hidden treasure. In reality, there probably was a system of sorts to keep people safe and out of the way of approaching armies throughout history. More than likely, it was a series of secret paths leading from one farm to another, hiding people in abandoned buildings along the way."

"So, did they really find anything?"

"Well, Grandpa told me they had just about given up. They were in their teens and working more and more. There was less time for running around the hills. They were supposed to be perfecting their pastry skills, not wasting time treasure hunting. That's when your great-grandmother died and left her farm and vineyard to Lydia.

"Grandpa accompanied Lydia to her farm for the funeral. This is where it gets interesting."

Pausing for more coffee, Mario looked at me. "Are you positive you've never heard any of this before?"

"Not at all. Why?"

"I just want to make sure you get the whole picture of how and what happened. That's all.

"It seems that while Grandpa and Lydia are at her mother's funeral services, they are approached by a strange old lady. Apparently, she told them she could see the future. They didn't believe her."

"Wait. I seem to remember something or some story about a psychic or an old woman who predicted things. I don't know if Grandma told me or if I read it in her journals. It didn't seem like she was a reliable person and I didn't pay a lot of attention to her."

"That's okay . . . no one was real sure about this lady, either. Some say she was related to some of the people living there, some say she was a crazy woman living in the hills, and some say she just went to every funeral to stir up people. Weird lady. But, she did get their attention when she brought a small music box with gold and jewels to Grandpa and Lydia after the service. She would give them the music box and a map to a castle if they would give her money."

"Really? That's how they acquired one of the music boxes? Is it one of mine? What about the map?" I have dozens more questions but Mario holds up his hand and I nod. I'll wait until he's finished.

"They paid her, took the music box and the map, and she disappeared. They never saw her again. In fact, no one did. It was like she was a ghost. But, their interest was sparked once again with thoughts of treasure. They figured the music box was worth something but really had no idea what.

"Shortly before they both had to go back to Venice to work, they decided to use the map to see where it took them. After all, they had made a similar map of this same area. Using the map they bought from the old woman, it led them to a worn out, crumbled building several kilometers away. Still on Lydia's mother's land, it probably was one of the buildings used by the owners of the castle.

It was there they discovered more than they ever thought possible in all their treasure hunting days.

"Keep in mind there wasn't a lot of fighting going on here during the war. Yet, people were afraid and did some strange things. According to Grandpa, if you had something of value and you didn't want the enemy to take it away, you'd hide it in the strangest place you could think of. Apparently, it had been that way for hundreds of years.

"This was a strange place for sure. I don't think anyone knew much about the old, rundown, overgrown castle overlooking the owner's vineyard. No one had ever mentioned who owned it. Now, the map led them to what was a crumbling pile of rocks. Just when they thought they had found something, it turned out to be just rubble."

"That had to be heartbreaking."

"It was. At least it was until they sat down to rest."

Chapter 24

Our morning was quickly turning into noon and Mario announced that he would continue on with the story once our lunch was served. He apologized for making me wait for lunch as my internal clock was surely asking for food by now.

During a delicious lunch of salad, bread, and wine, Mario continued.

"Keep in mind, I heard these stories from Grandpa when he was in his 90s. I don't know how much he remembered exactly as it happened. His maps have confirmed the places he mentioned, but he didn't keep detailed journals. That's why we need to read Lydia's to figure out if they are any more detailed or if they give us more information.

"Anyway . . . I think it was Grandpa who sat down to rest. The climb up to this castle was fairly long and the path was seriously overgrown. It was obvious no one had been here in a long time. Sitting down on what appeared to be one of the foundation stones, he rested his foot on the next stone, and it moved. Thinking they were loose and about to crumble some more, he got up to inspect.

"Sliding it just a little revealed an opening. He and Lydia managed to move it enough to see a small opening . . . big enough for a person to fit through. Having no light to peer into it, they decided one of them should try to crawl in and see what it was.

"This is where it gets kind of creepy."

"Creepy? I'm scared they get stuck."

"Right. Anyway, they do a little more looking around and find another stone along an adjacent wall that moves as well. Only this one moves easily and the opening to the space is much larger than they first thought. It's large enough for them both to fit and lets in the afternoon sunlight. They go for it.

"It turns out it's like a small room, only about five feet high and maybe 10 by 12 feet in size. The first thing they see is a skeleton."

"Yikes. A skeleton . . . as in a dead body? A human?"

"Yep. And, according to Grandpa, they almost left right then and there. And, it would have been a real shame to leave."

"Because . . . ?"

"Because they noticed a pile of stones and rubble in the corner. In that pile were two wooden boxes. Uncovering those boxes, they drug them out into the light and eventually up out of the lower room. One box held four small boxes . . . the music boxes."

"Four more? I thought we only had four total."

"I'll explain that part later. For now, they had four, plus the one they bought from the old woman at the funeral. They weren't real sure what they had, but they knew it had to be worth something. You see, in the second box was all kinds of jewelry, gemstones, and gold."

"Oh my. More than what I have?"

"I'm guessing it is your jewelry. And, now they had to get it all back to Lydia's house. Loading up their bags, they managed to get everything in except for the original wooden boxes. Figuring they would come back the next day and get those, they made their way back down the hilly slopes to Lydia's, dragging their bags with them. Saying nothing to her father or anyone else, they hid their stash in Lydia's luggage. She was in the process of moving to Venice to live in her family's villa and work at the pastry shop anyway, so any additional luggage would be just part of her things."

"Did they go back the next day?"

"Yes, they did. And, guess what? The wooden boxes were gone, the skeleton was gone, and the place looked like it had been ransacked even more than when they were there only a day before."

"What? Who would want a skeleton and old boxes? And, why tear up a place that's already a mess?"

"At that time, they didn't think a whole lot about it. Figured it was vandals or something. That is, until later."

"Later? What happened later?"

"Grandpa saw those wooden boxes."

Chapter 25

"What? What do you mean he saw the wooden boxes? I thought they were gone."

"They were gone from the castle on the hill but he saw them about a week later in Venice. He was accepting a delivery at Great-Grandpa's bakery and saw the boxes on the delivery man's boat."

"Are you sure they were the same ones? Was he sure they were the same ones?"

"Yes, he was positive. Since he knew the delivery man, he asked him where he got those boxes and was told a friend gave them to him. When he asked if he could buy them, the delivery guy told him he had another buyer who was paying big money for these old boxes. He was going to deliver them later."

"What happened to them? Did he ever see them again?"

"This is where it gets ugly. About a week later, Grandpa was accepting another delivery from the same company. The usual delivery guy wasn't there so Grandpa asked about him. He was curious about the boxes and wondered if he really did get big money for them.

"This delivery guy told him the regular delivery man was found in his apartment. His throat had been slit. According to what the police told him, nothing seemed to be missing."

"Oh my goodness. Did your grandpa think that was connected to the boxes?"

"At the time, he didn't. Years later, he knew they were connected."

"Really? How?"

"Let me fill you in on what Grandpa and Lydia did with the jewelry and the music boxes first.

"When they arrived in Venice from the hills, Lydia settled in to her parent's villa and started working for my great-grandfather in his bakery. She and my grandpa had decided to divide the music boxes. Grandpa took two plus the one they bought from the old woman, Lydia took two and all the jewelry. They were going to decide what to do with all of it as soon as they had time. They knew everything had to be of some value, so Grandpa hid his items in the attic. He had no idea where Lydia kept hers.

"Let's take a break. We've been sitting here most of the morning and I need to go to the market for our chef. If you want to come along, I can show you where your villa is. You can stay here tonight and then move there if you like."

"Good idea. I want to hear more, but I also want to see my villa. My villa. That sounds so unbelievable to me. Let me grab my purse, camera, and sketch pad. I took a sketching workshop and want to practice what I learned."

We head out the door, walk down a couple of streets, over a bridge or two, through a few alleys, and come out along the Grand Canal.

Wandering along the Rialto Fish Market, Mario tells me he needs to pick up some scallops. Nodding, I wander off to take photos of interesting looking fish, weird looking fish, giant squid, and baby octopi. Then I make my way to the fruits and vegetables section to shoot small purple artichokes, baskets of neon orange apricots, plump dates, containers overflowing with ripe, red berries, and odd shaped radicchio. Smells and colors bombard my senses and I lose myself in my photos. Such shapes and colors . . .

Suddenly, I am rudely and forcibly shoved toward the edge of the market. Figuring I bumped into someone while trying to get the perfect shot, I say excuse me as I turn around. No one is there but I see a man rushing off, only a couple of feet away. He turns to look back at me, just as Mario comes to my side. I swear that man looks like someone I've seen before. In fact, I know it.

He pulls his cap down over his eyes and disappears into the crowd.

"What was that all about?" asks Mario.

Looking back at the crowd and then at Mario I tell him, "I don't know, but something isn't right. I am positive I've seen that guy before . . . only I can't put my finger on when or where. He didn't just bump into me, either. He shoved me hard enough for me to lose my balance if I wouldn't have been braced to take a photo. And, he definitely didn't want to be seen. I need to think about his face. I'll see if I can sketch it when we get back to your place."

Just then my cell phone vibrates and I see I've missed a call from Clark.

Listening to his message, "Hope you're having a good time Just wanted to fill you in on a couple of things. There's been another development here. Call when you have time."

Looking around, Mario takes my arm. "Let's head back to my place. You can call Clark from there."

Chapter 26

Putting my phone down, I look at Mario as he brings an afternoon snack and some Prosecco out to the terrace.

"Clark says there has been another discovery of yet another music box like ours. This time in Milan. A fashion designer there had it and . . ." Stopping, I can't seem to finish the story without taking a deep breath.

Laying his hand on my shoulder Mario asks, "What is it, Marta? What happened?"

"He was killed sometime in the last week. His throat had been slit. When his girlfriend returned from Paris, she found him tied to one of their dining room chairs. Their place was messed up some, but the only thing she can think of that was missing was the music box. She had a special glass case made for it and displayed it in their living room. It was a gift he gave her on some anniversary. The girlfriend is pretty upset.

"Clark says Interpol is involved due to some fingerprints they found at the house. He also says, at some point we have to show our music boxes to them. The detectives in San Francisco are still involved but Interpol has now taken the lead."

Mario nods and says, "Let me finish what I know about the story and then we really need to read those journals and cookbooks. We must find out what Grandpa and Lydia knew or didn't know.

"It turns out Grandpa showed one of his music boxes to a trusted, or so he thought, baker. This baker had worked for his father for many years and he felt like he was more of an uncle than just another employee. Grandpa wanted to know if he had ever seen anything like this or where it might have come from in the beginning. The baker admired it but that was about it and Grandpa never gave it another thought.

"But, shortly after he showed him the box, it disappeared from Grandpa's room. You see, he had only brought one down from the attic and just hadn't taken it back there yet. And, this is the odd part . . . the baker left to go home two days later and never came back. He had worked for my great-grandfather for years. But, no one including my great-grandfather ever heard from him again. It was like he disappeared into thin air."

"Whoa. They had to be connected, don't you think? And, why do people keep disappearing or dying?"

Mario starts to answer and I interrupt him, "Wait a minute. Do you think we're in danger? Maybe that guy at the market was something more than a common thief who I thought was just after my purse. What's going on?"

"I wish I knew. But, I also wonder if we are in danger. No one knows you are here, do they?"

"Except the guy in the market, whoever he is. I made a crude sketch of his face. Not a great sketch but it was good practice."

"Yeah, right. I'm beginning to wonder more and more about him."

"Okay. What else did your grandpa tell you about the music boxes? And what about the jewelry? If I can believe the jeweler in San Francisco, it's just as valuable as the music boxes in its own right."

"That's about it. Grandpa hid his remaining two music boxes and told your grandmother to keep hers hidden. They were going to do more exploring as soon as they had time."

"So, what's brought about this sudden interest in these music boxes now? I mean, this was a long time ago. Right? Maybe if I get Grandma's journals and cookbooks, we can compare those to what your grandpa had written. Maybe we'll make sense of some of this. Then, we probably should contact Interpol as Clark suggested."

"Let's get all of our research done before we contact them. I feel better if we know what we're talking about before someone takes them away from us."

"Do you think they really would take them?"

"Yes, I do. So let's get to work. Unless you would like to catch a nap."

"No. I want to get some of this mystery solved. I'll stay here tonight and then you can show me my villa in the morning."

Chapter 27

Working while eating a tasty dinner, drinking some fantastic local wines, and sipping on after-dinner limoncello we began to make progress. Even if the dining room table looked like a pile of unorganized papers.

Grandma's cookbooks proved to be the key in all this. Starting with her journals, I quickly discovered those were where she wrote the changes she was going to make to recipes, where she kept her list of favorites, and everything else important to her baking. Apparently, those journals were more like notes to herself and not really diaries. Wonder why?

When I finally started looking at her cookbooks, it was obvious her notes along the side had to do with stories she heard about missing treasures, jewelry, and the music boxes. Apparently, those notes corresponded to the baker or chef or kitchen staff that was telling her the story. She included dates, how much she believed that person, and notes to herself to double check the facts. This was probably a handy place to make her notes, since she always had the cookbooks with her in the kitchen.

Since Mario's grandfather didn't keep many notes, we pieced together most of the puzzle from Grandma's cookbooks, Luigi's stories he told to Mario, and what little information we could get from the Internet.

Sitting back and organizing our notes and timeline I looked at Mario, "What did we ever do before the Internet? This research would take us days. And, we still might not have what we need."

"I know. At least we have a pretty good idea about the music boxes and their origin. We still aren't completely sure who really owned them and how they made it to the ruined castle on your great-grandmother's land."

"Right. It appears they may have originated in Yugoslavia or it Austria, commissioned by a duke or someone of royalty . . . if you look closely at the photos on the Internet. It does say there were at least ten of them at one time, given to important royal females. Their worth at that time was significant, so the jeweler I talked to in San Francisco was probably close in his original estimate.

"Grandma does mention Slavia and Serbia in her writings but that's about it. I have no idea if she's referring to the music boxes or just another story. Since we're not exactly sure of the dates they found the music boxes and jewelry, she could be talking about anything. I have no idea if there really was any treasure, according to these notes.

"I do wonder if her mother, my great-grandmother, knew they were there, though."

"Based on what I've read about history during that time and what Grandpa told me, I'd say someone who was afraid of all this being taken away during some war or change of leadership or something hid it all in a spot where they thought no one would look. This had to mean they somehow knew your great-grand-mother and knew she had an old castle in a remote area of the foothills. It also means they thought they could come back for it, which points again to them knowing her.

"Did she know it was there? I doubt it. After all, according to Grandpa, the place was almost completely destroyed. It was rubble. She wouldn't have left a couple of good sized boxes there, even if she thought they were just boxes. Nothing else was there."

Nodding, I agree. "Except, what about the old woman or psychic or whatever she was? How did she know they were there? Where did she get the map?"

"Good questions. Let's read some more and see if there is any mention of that in your grandma's notes."

Chapter 28

More notes, more tales about wealthy people hiding things, more stories that don't make sense, and more trips back and forth to the vineyards . . .

"I'm just about finished reading Grandma's notes in her cookbooks and nothing gives me any more clues. Do you have anything in the journals that helps us, Mario?"

"Well, I am seeing several references to a map. She keeps talking about the maps they made while she and Grandpa were exploring the vineyards as kids. She also mentions a book that she wants to keep hidden and safe. I'll keep reading. I'm almost finished and have only one more journal left to read. Are you done reading her cookbooks?"

"One left, but it doesn't have much writing in it that I can see.

"Whoa . . . on this page she writes about being afraid of a woman who came into the bakery early in the morning to see one of the kitchen staff. She describes her as hunched over, wearing loose clothing, and shuffling her feet. That wasn't what scared her, though. Apparently, the old woman came in, grabbed Grandma's coworker, hissed something in her face, and then looked right at Grandma. Her eyes were black and mean. That's exactly what she writes. Wait. There's more . . .

"Later that morning, Grandma apparently went to the market for some more fruit and saw the old woman again. This time the woman tried to grab Grandma with her bony fingers and missed. I'll read this part to you as Grandma writes it. 'Saw that nasty woman, twice in one day. Her eyes are the worst. They look into you with bad intentions. I got away but she hissed after me that she could see things and she knew where I kept my treasure. Since I don't have any treasure, I had no idea what she meant. When I got back to the bakery to ask Mary about her, I was told that Mary quit right after that nasty woman was here. Must find out more about the treasure.' That's it."

"So, that was apparently before she and Grandpa found the music boxes and jewelry. Does she have any dates on that entry?"

"Nope. Sorry. But it does kind of fit with the old woman they later encountered. And, it seems like none of these are in chronological order anyway. It's all so hard to sort out.

"She does have a couple of final entries and this appears to be the last cookbook. This one is underlined but again, no date. Wow. Listen to this . . . 'Check both maps again. Need to ask Dad about Mom and where she was born. Just heard a rumor from Giorgia that Mom's family was royalty. She told me I need to find my ancestors. Do you suppose our new found jewels really belong to me? Must talk to Dad. Maybe he knows about the book.'

"That's it. Now, I'm really curious. What maps? What book? How do we know what Great-Grandpa told her about Great-Grandma? How do we find out?"

Mario is nodding his head as he reads. "Well, that fits with this last journal post. She is reminding herself or maybe Grandpa that they were right when they made the castle map and the site map. And, guess who pointed them to the castle in the first place? Your great-grandmother, the owner of the castle and quite possibly the jewelry and music boxes. Apparently they thought they were looking for buried treasure left by someone else and all along it could have been owned and hidden by your great-grandmother."

"That also fits with what I have here. Let me read this last part to you . . . 'The site map has disappeared. Neither of us is forgetful so someone had to take it. It's a good thing we made a copy.

As soon as we can, Luigi and I will go talk to Mom about all the stories I'm hearing from Giorgia. We'll take our copy of that map and the castle map along and she can tell us what we should be looking for and where. Mom hasn't been well these last months, so we should get there in the next few weeks.'

"That's the very last entry. My guess is they never made it to talk to her before she died. Let's see if that fits with the time frame of talking to the old woman. And, let's see if my great-grandmother really did own the castle."

Chapter 29

"You're sure you don't have any more journals, maps, or relevant cookbooks back in San Francisco?" Mario looks at everything we have in front of us.

"Positive. Let's recap what we know.

"Grandma and Luigi were kids when they first heard stories about hidden treasures. As they got older, the stories became more exciting . . . not necessarily all true. During and maybe because of these, they made maps . . . again not sure if they are real or not.

"Great-Grandma or her family owned what appears to have been an old castle. We're not sure if she lived there or when it became destroyed. Grandma didn't really know her mother, it seems. Otherwise wouldn't she have stories from her? However, Great-Grandma was the one who suggested Grandma and Luigi go to the castle ruins, even though they never found anything on any of those jaunts.

"It was only after the old woman appeared at the funeral that Grandma and Luigi somehow stumbled upon the music boxes and jewelry. I still don't understand how or why she was involved, but there has to be some connection.

"Fast forward and we have music boxes surfacing and then disappearing again. Only this time, there are murders associated with them. Why? Who knows they exist? Who wants them? Are they valuable both in money and something else? Are all the murders connected? If so, shouldn't we be careful?

"Then, there's the jewelry. We haven't even learned anything about it."

All the while I'm talking and rambling, Mario is nodding his head and making notes. "Right on all counts. Clark is probably right as well. We need to contact Interpol. As nice as these music boxes are, they aren't worth dying over. And, we haven't even started looking up anything about the jewelry. Of course, no one has tried to steal it or died while connected to it. Maybe it's just valuable, old jewelry. I think we need to have it appraised piece by piece while you're here."

"I completely agree about Interpol and about getting the jewelry appraised. I only brought about half of it with me but we could start with that. Do you have some jewelers you trust?"

Starting to clean up my mess of cookbooks, journals, and maps, I flip Grandma's last cookbook over and add it to the pile when it falls apart. "Darn. I knew these were old and not in the best of shape, but I didn't mean to destroy this one."

Picking up the pages and placing them in order I start to lay them back in the cookbook. That's when I notice there is more to the front and back covers.

"Look, Mario. No wonder this cookbook is so heavy. The covers open up and there are more notes inside. And, a map. Do you suppose this is one of the maps they lost or is it something else? Maybe it's the special cookbook Grandma mentioned in the hospital.

"There are also what appear to be drawings. Oh dear, I've seen this crest before." Running to my room, I grab the brooch to show to Mario.

"Look, Mario. It's the same crest. Right?"

Mario has a puzzled look on his face as he studies the drawing of the crest. "This crest. I've seen it before. It's important but I can't think where I've seen it. And, your brooch matches perfectly.

It must be a family crest. Maybe this is the clue to owner of the jewelry."

"It should be easy enough to research on the Internet." My phone rings and I see it's Clark.

Chapter 30

Hanging up, I relate my conversation with Clark to Mario. "You'll never guess what's been going on in San Francisco. The police found Pete . . . dead. Apparently, they received a call from someone in his apartment complex about hearing gunshots. When they got there, they found him. They're checking the surveillance tape from the apartment's main entrance. Even though he seems to be a common thief, he apparently lived quite well in a very nice apartment."

"Do they have any motive?"

"Not yet, according to Clark. But, there's more.

"He had actual photos of several of the music boxes on his computer. Clark has verified my two as well as the missing ones from Giovanni and the man in San Diego. The FBI has a computer guy working on Pete's computer, trying to see if they can figure out where he got these photos. There were photos of other music boxes as well, but Clark had not seen those. He's emailing me those and we'll probably see your two in those photos."

"Does he say what we are to do with our music boxes?"

"Yes. In two or three days an agent with Interpol will be coming here to talk to us. In the meantime, we need to keep them safely hidden and make note of anything out of the ordinary that happens to either one of us. Plus, we are to stay here in Venice."

"Why? Do they think somebody knows what we have? Do they think someone is watching us?"

"I'm not sure. Clark had to hang up and will call back. He was with the FBI computer guy and apparently he found something more. That's it for now."

"Okay. We need a plan. Let's put the music boxes along with the jewelry in my safe and get a good night's rest. We can work on the jewelry in the morning."

"Oh . . . the map and papers I found in Grandma's cookbook. We should look at those. Except, I'm too tired to comprehend much more. Sleep is probably a good idea."

With dreams of bright jewels and the old, ugly woman, I still manage to sleep quite well.

Chapter 31

Sitting out on the terrace enjoying my morning coffee and tasty pastries, I thought I could really get used to this. Reflecting back on the last several months, I can't believe how things have changed. What I thought I knew . . . I didn't have a clue. When I figured I knew all about Grandma . . . it appears I didn't have a clue there, either. Nothing is as it seems.

Wait a minute. Isn't that what that note said . . . the one I received before all the pieces started to fit? Where is that note? I know I put it with my things to bring here after the detectives gave it back to me. Retrieving it from my notebook, I look at it again just as Mario brings a tray of fruit to our table.

"Mario, look at this note. It came to me sometime before everything started happening. The detectives couldn't find any fingerprints on it or on the envelope. That part was odd. When the detectives asked me about the delivery guy, what he looked like, and what he was wearing, I filled them in on what I could remember. At the time, I was so annoyed he was looking into my house and interrupting me. When I sat and really thought about him, he was not memorable. Probably by design. His clothes were nondescript, he had no company uniform, he wore gloves which

I thought was strange, and his hat was pulled down over his eyes just like . . .

"Oh my goodness. At the time this didn't come to me but . . ." Squeezing my eyes shut, I can just about see him.

"What is it? You look like you've seen a ghost. Are you okay?"

"The guy. That delivery guy reminds me of the man at Grandma's bedside in the hospital. And, now that I really concentrate, I can see him"

"Who? Who can you see?"

Taking a deep breath and opening my eyes, "There was a man in the hospital when Grandma was dying; right there in her room. He walked right by her bed and looked at her. When he caught me looking at him, he disappeared. I was going to go after him and ask how he knew my grandma, as I had never seen him before. Then Grandma started talking to me and giving me warnings. And, then she died. I never thought any more about that man.

"But, weeks later two delivery guys bring two envelopes to me at different times. I'm not positive, but I think they were the same man. Neither time did either man have a company uniform. I didn't even connect them to the guy in the hospital until now."

Mario starts to ask a question and I tell him to give me a minute.

"If I think hard enough . . . the guy in the market who shoved me . . . reminds me of the other ones. Not just in his build, but his mannerisms and facial features. He had his hat pulled down but I could still see his jaw line and his snarly smile. Yes, I'm almost positive they are all the same guy."

"Okay. You need to call Clark and fill him in on this. I think things just got worse."

"You're right. Oh, here's the note I received. What do you think about it?"

Nothing is at it seems. Trust no one. Be careful. They are watching you.

Chapter 32

Handing it back to me, "Well, I think several things. First, if the delivery guy isn't a good guy or is out to harm you, why would he give you a warning?"

"Yeah, I thought the same thing. But, maybe he didn't know what was in the envelope. Maybe someone hired him to deliver it."

"Second, are you quite certain these guys all could be the same person?"

"Yes. The hospital guy and the market guy and the delivery guys all have the same look. And, I don't think it's just the hat. I can picture them with their square jaw line and thin, nasty smiles."

"Okay. They could actually be just a guy hired to hang around, deliver letters, and scare you. Someone else might be behind all this. After all, we are talking about murders, too."

"Right. But . . . Grandma's attorney is the one who sent the first letter. The one from Grandma. I called him. It was a legitimate letter and scheduled to be delivered to me on a certain date. The attorney didn't know which service was going to deliver it, however."

"And, you're sure these guys didn't have uniforms from some reliable delivery service?"

"Their clothes were all gray. No markings and no logos. I didn't see their trucks, however. So, they could have come from a company I am not familiar with or some private delivery service. That's not uncommon."

"Okay. Let's think about the note. Has Clark seen it?"

"No. But, the detectives have seen it and examined it."

"I think Clark should see it as well. It's clearly a warning, but from whom?"

"I don't know. Maybe we should start on the jewelry and see if things clear up at all. I'll let Clark know about the note when he calls later today."

"Good idea. I have the jewelry laid out on the dining room table so we can research each piece separately. We can also look into the pieces still at your home, using the photos you have. You asked if I knew a reliable jeweler. I have contacted a trusted friend to come here this afternoon. He's a jeweler and a collector. He'll be able to shed some light on what you have. Then, we need to go to your villa. Even if you want to continue to stay here, you must be anxious to see it."

"I am. Let's go there right after lunch. Maybe we should walk by the market again to see if we see the same guy who shoved me."

"I'm not sure that's a good idea . . . the market that is. We can decide that later. Right now, let's start on the jewelry."

Having no idea how old the jewelry is created a few problems when trying to find out about it. We also discovered that if this was a private collection, we might never know much about it. We found other old pieces that were documented and written about, but not these. Thinking I might have better luck looking for a collection rather than individual pieces, I start down that path. Just then it hits me . . . I need to get the maps and cookbook from last night. I had forgotten about those.

Grandma hid or kept several documents in the covers of this cookbook for a reason and it took some time piecing them together. Mario was working on different pieces of jewelry while I tried to figure out what Grandma was trying to tell me.

Looking at two detailed maps, they appear to be just that. Detailed drawings of vineyards, hills, and other structures are clearly marked. One map refers to a castle, but doesn't say anything about it or why she marked it. Nothing gives me any indication these maps were ever used for anything. Yet, I wonder why she went to the trouble to hide them inside the covers of the cookbook.

Next, I start on the pages of notes she has with them. Interesting, as I gain more insight into Grandma's life as a teen-ager and at the start of her pastry chef career. But, nothing that gives me the information I was hoping to find. And, again I wonder why she went to the trouble to hide these. Finished reading, I look at the cookbook again, wondering why I never noticed the covers before.

Checking inside the front and back covers one last time, a smaller paper is wedged along the bottom. It probably became stuck as she shoved all this in here. Not wanting to rip it, gently I remove it. The old cover tears a little and I feel badly for destroying part of Grandma's prized possessions.

Unfolding it, several things immediately jump out at me.

Chapter 33

"Mario, look at this. I have a paper with a code, some dates, and names. It also says the word chest on it. What on earth?"

"Where did you get that?"

"This small piece of paper was stuck in the back of the cover. I wonder if Grandma put it there on purpose. It's fragile and I'm afraid it will fall apart. But, look. I wonder what these numbers and names mean. They could be names of people or towns, for all I know. Some almost look like dates written next to pieces of jewelry.

"Look, one place she writes the word 'necklace' after her numbers. Oh look. She has the word 'ring' written here and the word 'stone' written here. Do you suppose it somehow corresponds to the jewelry? That could be why your grandpa didn't have anything like this. She kept all the jewelry. Right?"

"That would make sense. We need to inventory your jewelry and then maybe it will make more sense."

"Let's see if these dates mean anything. You will be better with those as you have a better feel for when your grandpa started working and when he and Grandma went exploring."

"Okay. Let me start a timeline of dates and see what she has written."

"I'll look up the names on the Internet to see if I can get any history on them. For all we know, they could be names of her pets."

Researching names and dates brought us one step closer to making a time line and making sense of what happened during that time. But, we still didn't have anything that mentioned jewelry. And, none of the names were any we had ever heard. It seems there were names written that could have been first or last names. We also had no idea how Grandma and Luigi would have been involved in any of this.

"Why did she keep these names, dates, and this odd code? I go back to the fact that it must have meant a great deal to her or she wouldn't have gone to all the trouble to keep it hidden."

"I'm getting nowhere, either. Sure, I have a bunch of information. Nothing that is anything more than a detailed history lesson, however. Let's take a break. Our cook has lunch ready. Then we can go see your villa. Who knows . . . maybe we'll find something there."

Chapter 34

My villa. Even though Mario said that's where we were headed, it's hard to comprehend I have a place in Venice. Off we go. Down a couple of alleys we head over another bridge and round a corner as Mario points to the one with the double arches I saw from Emilio's boat. Not huge like some of the villas and palaces I've seen, it's perfect.

"It's spectacular. And, it's all mine."

Rising three stories from the street, it sits just one or two small canals off the Grand Canal. It's quiet with not a lot of foot traffic. Of course, most of Venice is quiet in a way no other city is. The soft green marble façade is welcoming and the double arch entryway gives character to the entire front.

"It's mine. I can't believe it."

"Here's the key. Let's go inside. Your grandma hired a small staff when she was here and they have instructions to get it ready for you anytime you want to visit."

"Really? Do they live here?"

"Not all of them. There is a maid service that comes in weekly and if you want more staff, they will stay. You can have a cook if you want."

Excited, I'm getting my first glimpse of how Grandma lived here in Venice. Opening first the metal door and then the carved wooden doors, a small entry way is lit by a modest, yet sparkling chandelier. In front of us is a flight of old, stone steps. Making our way up those steps, the first floor is lit by a grander, two tiered chandelier. Tasteful yet stunning, the crystal chandelier sparkles as it lights up the entire foyer on this level. I turn to tell Mario how excited I am, only he's no longer standing beside me. He has gone back downstairs.

I go back down and join him as he is outside staring at the doors in the entry way.

"Mario, what's wrong? What are you looking at?"

"I can't believe it never registered until now. I knew I remembered that symbol, but I couldn't put my finger on where I had seen it. It's right here. This has to be a sign of some sort. I need to compare it to your brooch to be sure."

"What the hell are you talking about? What symbol?" Then it hits me, too. Stamped into the metal work on the front door is what looks like a crest. It certainly appears to resemble the crest on one of my gold brooches. "I see it now. But, let's keep looking through my villa before we go back to bring the brooch here. Okay?"

"That's fine. We might see something else. And, I'm not sure what this is telling us, other than they are the same crest or symbol. Did we ever find this symbol on the Internet?"

"No, although there appear to be similar ones."

"From what I saw, it seems there are plenty of family crests, but most weren't famous or notable. If a family had a crest, it was used on their property. But, it didn't mean they were wealthy or royalty or anything. It was just for family use.

"Still, we might find the brooch and this crest were connected. But for now, let me show you the rest of the villa."

Finishing our tour overwhelms me and saddens me a little. How I wish I could have been here with Grandma. It's not an opulent place, but certainly a villa by anybody's standards. I want to stay here but not until we figure out what's going on with the music

94

boxes and the jewelry. Now that we've seen the same crest on the front door and woven into the rug in the small room that belonged to Great-Grandma, we're both convinced it means something.

Walking down the staircase in front of me, Mario holds up his hand. "I might know someone who would know a little about this crest. Grandpa had a friend who built boats for wealthy people. His son or grandson took over his business. It seems like they always knew everything about everyone. He would be a good person to ask if he's ever seen this before. If not, no harm. But, if it did belong to somebody important or wealthy, he would probably know."

"Do you think we could take a picture of this door or the rug and show it to him? Is he far from here? Maybe we should go now before we try to do any more research."

"Good idea. You brought your camera. Let's take some photos and head to his place. It's off the Grand Canal. We can take the vaporetto to the stop a short ways from his shop."

Chapter 35

Talking with Alfonso, the boat builder, we learn a little more and now we have more questions. It certainly seems like this puzzle will never end.

Bringing out a book showcasing boats his family built throughout the centuries, immediately he pointed to the drawing of a crest that matches the photos I show him on my camera. He recognized the crest right away as that of a family of importance, possibly royalty. This family had their crest embroidered on the seat backs of the boat his great-grandfather built for them. According to the notes, it was a finely crafted boat and money was no object.

I wasn't sure how he could recognize this one so quickly until he asked us a question.

"It's amazing. What are the odds you would be the second people to ask about this very same crest in the matter of a week?"

In unison Mario and I ask, "What? What do you mean?"

Seeing our shock, Alfonso holds up his hand. "One day last week two men came in with a photo of this same crest. They insisted on looking through several of my books. When they found the one they were looking for, they asked me all kinds of questions about it. It was obvious by my responses that I was just a baby when this boat was built. I could really tell them nothing other than what they read of Great-Grandpa's notes. That's why I recognized so quickly those photos of yours. I had just seen it."

"What kind of questions?" Mario gets out his notebook.

"Let's see. They wanted to know when it was built, who built it, who paid for it, where it is now, who owns it, and if it is still functioning. Then, this was strange. They asked if anyone else had asked me about this crest or this boat. Now that you're asking, maybe it wasn't so strange."

"Would you know them if you saw them again? What did they look like?" Hoping one of them was the market guy or delivery guy, I pulled out my sketch pad and showed my crude sketch to Alfonso.

"No. That wasn't either one of them. Both of them had larger faces than that. They were big guys, dressed in black, and had an air of authority about them. I think they were used to telling people what to do by the way they talked to me."

"Okay. By the way, do you know the family name? If so, did you give it to the other two guys also?"

"Yes, I have a name and yes I gave it them. They acted like they already knew that name, however. So, I'm not exactly sure what they really wanted me to do other than confirm everything. The name that Great-Grandpa has written here is Sante. I'm not sure if he meant that as a family name or not. His notes are hard to decipher. Why? Does that mean something to you as well?"

Both of us shook our heads. "No, I'm afraid it doesn't. But it is one more piece of the puzzle we can add to our growing pile. It is curious, though, that this same crest would be on a brooch Grandma had, in her family's villa, and then on a boat built specifically for some family. Right?"

Mario agreed, "It's most certainly an important piece. We'll have to keep looking. Thanks again Alfonso. We appreciate your help."

Turning to leave, Mario has one last thought, "Alfonso, would you give me a call if anyone else comes here asking about this crest?"

"No problem. In fact, that's what the two guys said when they left."

"What? Did they give you a number to call?"

"They did. I don't know why I didn't think of it until now. Let me get their card."

Mario and I look at each other in anticipation as Alfonso comes out of his office. Handing Mario the card, "Here is the card they gave me. I didn't really look at it until now. You can have it."

"What the hell?" Stunned, Mario hands me the card to look at.

"Oh my goodness." I can't even think what we should be doing next.

Chapter 36

"Leaving Alfonso's place with the card in hand, Mario and I are still in shock.

"Mario, what does this mean? Do we call them? Can we be sure these two men are really from Scotland Yard? Better question . . . why is Scotland Yard involved?"

"Marta, I have no idea. I think we need to get back to my place and call Clark. He seems to have his hand on a lot of what's going on. Maybe he can shed some light on all of this.

"One thing we do know, the jewelry plays an important part. I almost forgot. Sam is coming by to look at your jewelry in about an hour."

"Sam?"

"Yeah, I know. Odd name for an Italian jeweler, huh? Actually he comes from a long line of jewelers. When his ancestors came to Italy from Austria, they all changed their names. I have no idea what his real name is. I call him Sam. He has proven to be a valuable asset to me when evaluating my music boxes and other family heirlooms. He's a good guy and we can trust him. Let's go see what he has to say about your jewelry."

Hurrying to Mario's, we arrive the same time Sam does. Mario introduces me and as he and Mario catch up, I gather all the jewelry I brought to Italy with me and lay it out on the dining room table once again. Even though I only brought about half, it still fills the table sparkling in the light from the windows and the chandelier.

"Wow. What a nice collection. I assume this is what you want me to look at, Mario?" Sam brings out a soft cloth and gently picks up one piece, holding it up to the light. Using his jewelers loupe, he examines it first in sunlight and then with a small flashlight. Moving on, he silently examines each piece while we both watch.

I'm almost afraid to breathe, let alone speak.

He is seriously quiet, almost reverent as he lays each piece back on the table.

When he's finished he says, "I have some questions. And, then I want to look at it all again. Okay?"

We both nod. And I speak, "First of all, thank you for coming to Mario's. We had no idea what we should do about this. I had a couple pieces appraised in San Francisco, but I'm not sure I like or trust the jeweler there. Please, ask your questions and we'll tell you what we know."

"These are exquisite pieces, amazing workmanship. And, very old. Where did you get them? Do you know who they belonged to? Please tell me what you know about this collection."

"My grandma and Mario's grandpa found them in an old building on my great-grandmother's property when they were just teen-agers. They found the music boxes you already know about and this jewelry. This is about half of what I have. The rest is in San Francisco in a safe."

"Good. I'm glad it's in a safe." Sam interrupts me. "Go on, please."

"We've been trying to research and find similar pieces but without much luck. Then, there's this brooch with a family crest or something on it. We found the same design in the front door and on a rug in my grandma's villa.

"We also just came from a boat builder who built a boat for the family who had the same design used on their boat. The weird part of that is, there were two supposed Scotland Yard men at the boat builders last week asking about this design."

"What did your jeweler in San Francisco say about the jewelry?"

"He was mesmerized by the music box, so his focus was on that. He did tell me the pieces I took to him were probably associated with royalty and were worth in the neighborhood of several hundred thousand US dollars. I didn't tell him I had more jewelry or a second music box."

I start to ask a question and my phone rings. It's Clark.

"Excuse me, I should take this and see what he has to say. I'll also tell him about the two men and ask what he knows about Scotland Yard. In fact, let me put him on speaker and we can all talk to him."

"Clark, it's good to hear from you. I have you on speaker as we have questions and some additional information. What do you have to tell us?"

"Marta, Mario . . . it's not good news. The jeweler you had appraise your pieces here in San Francisco is missing. His shop was ransacked and several items are missing. Curiously, all of his files were taken but not all of his high end jewelry. Marta, your file was in there, wasn't it? The SFPD found partial fingerprints that they matched to a jewel thief wanted in England. Now we have Scotland Yard involved."

"Clark, Scotland Yard was here, too."

"What do you mean, 'here'?"

"It's a long story."

Chapter 37

As I start to explain our day to Clark, he interrupts, "Who is Sam?"

At the same time, Sam asks, "Clark. Is that really you?"

Mario and I look at each other as it dawns on us that the other two know each other. Explaining, Sam tells us he has worked with Clark on high end jewelry heists in the past. It seems they have a mutual admiration society by the way they're both telling us we have the right guy working with us.

We talk some more and then decide it's best if Clark comes to Venice bringing the rest of my jewelry. Mario offers to send his plane, but Clark assures us he can get special clearance to fly first class and keep the jewelry safe. He'll have Agent Lynne, one of the SFPD detectives, stay at my house with Shadow and to keep an eye on anything happening in the neighborhood.

Sam has been looking more closely at my jewelry and tells Clark he'll have more information by the time he gets here. "I'm going to go to my shop and do some more research. I know I've seen some of this before, or at least some pieces that remind me of this collection. I'll gather all I can and meet everyone back here in two days when Clark gets here.

"For now, I want to snap some photos to take with me. I want you to keep the jewelry here in Mario's safe. I have a feeling it is somehow tied to the music boxes, especially since Luigi and your grandma found them together."

"Okay. I think I should explore my villa some more. I'm not exactly sure there are any clues there. But, I would like to investigate it a little more."

Mario nods. "I'll go with you. We can look around and come back here for dinner. Okay?"

Finished taking photos of my jewelry, Sam wraps it all back up and takes it to Mario's safe. "I'll see you both in a couple of days. Let me know if you find anything at the villa. Maybe we should take a trip up to your winery when Clark gets here. We may stumble upon something there . . . or at least drink some of your fantastic Prosecco."

"I was thinking the same thing", says Mario. "We should at least look at the place where all this started. After Clark gets here, let's take a road trip."

"Sounds like a plan." Sam leaves and we head back over to my villa.

"I still can't believe Grandma had all this jewelry and the music boxes and I didn't know anything about them. Why didn't she tell me? We used to talk about so much but, never this. And, why did she think to warn me only as she was dying? The more I think about what she said, the clearer it is to me that those were real warnings. But, warnings of what? What did she know that she felt compelled to warn me about?"

"You're right. Those had to be warnings. I wonder what triggered them then. Did she see something or someone?"

"Wait. Remember, the hospital guy reminded me of those delivery guys? I don't remember if I saw him before or after she warned me, though. Do you suppose she saw him and it triggered a memory?"

"Could be. We'll never know. Let's take an inventory of everything we see here at your villa."

Chapter 38

After a couple hours of systematically working our way through all corners of my villa, taking inventory, making notes, and opening every drawer neither of us are any closer to finding anything out of the ordinary. This is a well-stocked, well taken care of home. Just as we decide this is a fantastic place to live but there's nothing here to help us in our search, the front door bell rings. We both go see who is there.

Introducing herself as Millie, she tells us she was a friend of Grandma's when they were both living and working here in Venice. She tells us she's about 10 or so years younger than Grandma and always looked up to her at the bakery where she was a junior apprentice when Grandma was a baker. Looking closely at her, she could pass for even younger than that. Stylishly dressed, with her snow white hair perfectly cut and coiffed, and enough jewelry to start her own store, Millie excuses herself for stopping by unannounced.

Welcoming her inside, she looks around and says, "I always loved this place. Your family took such good care of it once they bought it. So many places in Venice have deteriorated dramatically. Lydia would invite me here with some of the other bakers after we finished our work. We'd sit out on the terrace and listen to stories from the older chefs and bakers. Nothing like getting a history lesson firsthand. Of course, your grandma always served the best treats and the very best Prosecco!"

"That's kind of you. The villa is mine now and we were just looking around. I'm staying at Mario's until I decide what I want to do."

"I don't think you should sell this. You could always rent it out. A lot of Venetians are doing that, you know. Before you do that, make sure you find all of Lydia's hidden passageways and treasures. She was quite the master at that."

"What?" Mario and I ask in unison.

"I'm sure she must have told you stories about this place."

"Not really. I think we should sit and have some Prosecco and you can fill us in."

"Well, if you insist. I could have just one glass. I was so sorry to hear of Lydia's passing. She was a true lady, with a mischievous spirit thrown in. Please tell me she didn't suffer."

"I was at her bedside. She had only been in the hospital a short while and really only sick for a very short time. Only a month before that she had been to visit me in San Francisco. I could tell she was failing, but I didn't really know how sick she was. She never let on. And, I'm so glad she didn't have to suffer at all.

"You mentioned her treasures and some passageways. Mario and I are trying to piece together some history of some items she left me in her will. I had never seen them before and wanted to know more about them."

Nodding, Millie sips her Prosecco. "Your grandmother, she was a character when she wanted to be. All the old chefs and bakers would tell us younger ones stories. I'm sure most of those stories were made up, but that didn't stop Lydia and Luigi from going off on their treasure hunts."

"Did you ever have a chance to go with them?"

"No. I was too young. For me, it was fun listening to them talk about their adventures. There was the one time they came back from the vineyards all excited about something. They wouldn't share it with us, even though we begged and begged.

They said they had secrets. I think it was when they went to Lydia's mother's funeral."

"Did you ever find out what they found?"

"Oh my yes. I wasn't about to let that drop. Lydia practically danced when she came back. A few weeks after the funeral, Lydia asked if I wanted to come home with her. She told me she had something to show me. Of course, wild horses couldn't keep me away.

"That's when she showed me her secret hiding places."

Chapter 39

Full of questions, I rapid fire them at Millie.

"What places? Could you show us? What did she hide there? What did she show you?"

Millie just giggles as she holds up her hands. "Slow down. I'm not as young as I once was. First, let me tell you what she wanted to show me. Then, I'll see if I remember where those places were.

"Lydia and Luigi had somehow stumbled upon some real life treasure. Lydia talked about a strange old lady they met. Apparently, she told them she was a psychic or something, I think. But, we didn't really believe in them. She was probably just somebody that liked to think she was mysterious. In reality, she probably hung out at a tavern and picked up information or lies from the locals after they had too much to drink.

"Anyway, they found these boxes. I seem to remember they were hidden, or buried, or something along those lines. They were full of jewelry and some little, fancy music boxes. What really excited Lydia was the family crest she found. You see, it matches the one on the front door and on one of the rugs in her mother's bedroom and somewhere in the wallpaper here in this villa."

Nodding and not wanting to interrupt Millie now, we both tell her to continue.

"I guess Lydia was sad at first about her mother. Although, I had the impression she never really knew her because she certainly didn't talk about her much. This is where it gets confusing to me. Maybe I just don't remember it all very well.

"There was something about Lydia's father after her mother died. I don't think he lived very long afterwards. I can't remember." Millie pauses to enjoy her Prosecco and a piece of melon.

"That's okay. I don't know much about either of them. Grandma didn't really talk about them. And, just recently I found out I inherited the land from my great-grandmother and the half of the winery and property in the vineyards.

"And, we have seen the crest. We didn't know anything about it, who it represented, or what the family name was. We are hoping to find out more since it's what I inherited from Grandma. We're both thinking it has to be a clue to something."

"Oh it is. Lydia asked her father about it and all he would say is that it was a secret. Her mother's secret. She was so frustrated with him at that point. I know she and Luigi talked to some people at the bakery about it. Lydia told me there was one old Austrian guy who came into the bakery a few times every year. He lived in Trieste and came to Venice to visit his daughter. He always wore a jacket with a very ornate, distinctive crest on the pocket.

"Lydia figured he would know something about her crest or at least be able to tell her what it represented. He did. And, that's why Lydia devised the hiding spots."

"Now you have my attention. Maybe we're getting somewhere. I would love to know about this crest. Would you like another glass, Millie? I know I need one."

"Well, maybe just a small glass. Thank you."

"You're welcome. Please continue."

"I wasn't at the bakery when Lydia talked to him so I really don't know all the particulars. But, I do remember what Lydia told me when she showed me her brooch and her hiding spots.

"She said the man from Trieste was related to a Duke, I think. Royalty of some type, anyway. This was in the old Austrian or Hungarian time. Not real recent, apparently. He looked at Lydia's brooch frontwards and backwards and told her it was definitely a royal crest. He couldn't remember which family, though. He was trying to pick up the name from the design as some families did that. They hid their names in the gold work. But, he couldn't get a complete name. He did say the family name most likely started with an 'S'.

"Anyway, he had a whole book showing all the different crests. He was going to bring it the next time he came to Venice. But that didn't happen."

"Why? Did he forget it?"

"No. Sadly, he died on his way back to Trieste that trip. I seem to remember Lydia saying something about an accident. She was so upset that she wouldn't know any more about the crest."

"Darn. I was hoping he was our key. I guess we'll keep looking."

Millie set her glass down and asked, "Do you want to see the hiding spots? That is . . . if I can remember where they were."

"By all means. I was so wrapped up in the story, I forgot about those. Please show us where to look."

Chapter 40

Following Millie through my villa, I saw it through the eyes of a young woman. We discovered places my grandma had either found or created, places where she loved to entertain, and places she hid special things. Who knew she was so sneaky and so interested in hiding things?

Millie found three unique spots Grandma had shown her. Small spots, no one would see them unless you knew they were there. Actually, they were more like secret drawers and hidden shelves. And, we found nothing in them.

Now, Millie tells us she must leave. Thanking her for showing us around the villa, we make our way back down to the terrace. She picks up her handbag and stops in mid stride. "Wait. I remember. Just a minute. Let me think."

Closing her eyes, she is almost motionless. Mario and I look at her and then at each other.

"Yes. I seem to remember one more spot. Lydia didn't show it to me more than once, I believe. What did she say about it? Something about this spot being special, even her father didn't know about it. At one time, she was big into learning about her mother. Then, after her father died . . . she just stopped talking about it.

"Of course, about that time, she met your grandfather in a hospital in Verona. She would go there and volunteer in the kitchen about once a month. She never forgot him or quit talking about him, for that matter. I think she fell in love the first time she met him." Millie seems to be remembering that quite well, so I direct her back to the last hiding place she was talking about.

"Oh right . . . I get carried away sometimes. Yes, Lydia was so proud of this spot. You see, she said she finally understood something about her mother. I'm not sure what it was, but it did have something to do with where her mother came from."

"Really? Where did her mother come from and what else did she tell you?" I am so full of questions.

"I really have no idea where her mother came from or why it was so important to Lydia to know anything about it. I thought she said they had land up around Conegliano or Valdobbiadene where she and Luigi would go some times. That's not all that different. Maybe I just don't remember it quite right."

"Millie, that's okay. But, do you remember about the spot Grandma showed you? Do you think you could find it again?"

"Of course. I may be old but I'm not senile." With that, she giggled again.

Mario and I looked at her and smiled. We couldn't help but love and enjoy this lady.

"Let's go upstairs to Lydia's bedroom. Did you notice how everyone had their own bedrooms and dressing rooms? I just love the way this villa has been restored." We all head back upstairs once again. I'm thinking we've been over every square inch of Grandma's bedroom at least twice. What could we have possibly overlooked? I'm also thinking a secret hiding spot wouldn't be so secret in your bedroom. Wouldn't people look there first? Oh well, I'll keep my thoughts to myself as we follow behind Millie.

Millie stops just inside the doorway and closes her eyes once more. "We were sitting in her chairs overlooking the canal. Lydia was excited about something and I guess I was the one she decided to confide in about her latest secret. She made me promise not to tell anyone until she could figure it all out. But, I guess you two don't count. She wouldn't care now."

"I'm sure Grandma would want us to know whatever it is she told you. Please continue." I glance at Mario and he looks at me like we need to prod Millie a little more. She does get carried away reminiscing.

"Right. Let's see. She laid a second brooch, I think it was, on the table in front of me. She said it belonged to her great-grandma or great-great-grandma. I'm not sure. It was gold filigree filled with gemstones, only this time I think it had a complete name and not just the letter 'S' in the middle."

"What? A second one? Where did she get this one?"

"I can't quite remember but I think she said it was in a box of clothes and things her mother had stored here at the villa. Have you found that, yet? Her father was staying full-time at the vineyard farm by now and I think Lydia wanted to show him these things. I don't think she ever had the chance, however."

"Why is that? I don't know much about either of Grandma's parents."

"I'm pretty sure he died shortly after her mother died. At least that's what I remember. Anyway, Lydia looked through her mother's things and found this second brooch. It was a lot larger and much more ornate than the first one she had shown us all at the bakery.

"I know she wanted to find out if the name on it was her mother's maiden name, but I have no idea if she ever did."

"What was the name?"

"I think it was Sante."

Chapter 41

"Sante. Isn't that the same name the boat guy told us? I wonder what that means. Do you think it's still here? Millie, do you remember where the hiding spot was?"

Stepping into Grandma's bedroom suite, Millie turns and smiles at us. "Why, of course. Lydia wanted no one to take any of this away. I think it was all she had from her mother.

"Come over here and help me."

Millie walks to the rather large closet, opens both doors, and pulls up the corner of the rug. Mario helps her carefully roll it towards the back wall. There on the floor is a small latch embedded into the floorboard. No one would see it or if they did, they wouldn't think anything of it. It just looks like one of the lines and marks on the wooden floor. Mario looks at Millie and she nods.

"Here, pull here. Then turn it. This is what Lydia showed me."

Pulling the latch up, Mario turns it in the direction Millie indicated. A loud click and the trap door beneath slowly raises up a couple of inches. Only about two feet square, it's easy for Mario to raise the door up all the way and lock it in place.

Sitting in this dark, hidden spot is a box similar to mine in San Francisco; the one that held the music boxes. Inlaid with mother-of-pearl, gold, and silver on its shiny black top, a mountain scene is depicted in great detail.

Millie claps her hands like a little child on Christmas morning. "Yes. That's it. Isn't that just the most beautiful workmanship? I loved looking at it when Lydia showed it to me and it looks just the same now. I wondered if it would still be here."

"You said this was from Grandma's mother, right? It's curious that it is so similar to mine back home."

Mario is lifting it out of its hiding spot and asks, "Where did you get yours? It wasn't with the things they found in the rubble."

"It was in one of the boxes Grandma had delivered to me after she died. Her letter to me didn't mention where it came from or how she happened to have it. In fact, she didn't mention anything about it. Just about the music boxes and the jewelry."

"Millie, you said Lydia found this one in her mother's things. Right?"

"That's what I remember her saying. She mentioned a trunk or chest with old clothes, this box, and a larger brooch thingy. The rest is kind of fuzzy. I only saw this box one time."

"I wonder what happened to the clothes, the trunk, and the brooch or whatever it was. Let's open this box and see what Grandma put in here to hide."

Sitting on a small table in front of the window, the box shines magnificently in the late afternoon sun. Running my hand over the smooth top, "Mine has a Venetian scene with gondolas and canals on it. Other than that, they could be a matched set."

Millie's wide-open eyes and startled expression catch my eye. "What is it, Millie?"

"Look. Look at the castle on the mountainside. It has an 'S' on it, doesn't it? And, it reminds me of a painting hanging downstairs in the den. Did you see that one?"

"Not really. We can look at that later. Right now I need to unlock this and see what was so important that it had to be hidden."

Like mine, the key was attached to the bottom. And, like mine, the contents caught our attention. When the lid opened we all gasped.

Chapter 42

Black velvet, rich and soft, lined the interior of the box. But that's not what we focused on. Nestled into the velvet darkness was a simple tiara, alive with sparkling diamonds. Next to it lay an ornate crest, similar yet larger than the brooch I already have. Gold, like mine, this one has a word written in the middle of it. It could be Sante.

None of us moved a muscle. Millie was the first one to speak.

"Is this what I think it is?"

Nodding, Mario and I looked at each other. "We think so. Or, at least if you mean does this look like something a royal family would wear . . . then, yes."

Millie nodded, "I wonder why they kept them hidden. Wouldn't you want to share these with people? Or, wait a minute . . ." Again closing her eyes, we wondered if she was remembering something else.

"Millie, are you okay? What is it?"

"The painting. The one in the dining room. You've seen it, right?"

"I'm sure I've seen every painting here but obviously I need to look at them again. Why? What are you seeing, Millie?"

"I'm positive there is a painting of a woman sitting by a canal. She has this tiara on her head. I know it. I never thought to ask Lydia who it was in the painting and Lydia didn't tell me. Then, there's the painting in the den of a castle on a hill in some vineyards. I think it has an S on its door or somewhere. We need to look at those."

"Just a minute. First I want to look at this tiara and the crest or whatever it is." Carefully lifting both of them out of the box, the crest is heavy. Not really a brooch someone would wear, it's more like a showpiece. I'm not sure where you would display it. The large word in the middle is obviously meant to be recognized. Surrounded by red stones, possibly rubies, it's an imposing piece.

Then there is the tiara. Delicate yet stunning, this is a piece meant for royalty. Holding it up to the light, the diamonds sparkle, sending dancing prisms all around the room. I'm thinking Shadow would love chasing them up and down the walls. "I wonder whom this belonged to. Did Grandma ever show this to you or mention it to you, Millie?"

"No. She just showed me the box and I figured that was enough of a wonderful piece. I did wonder why she kept it hidden here in this spot. There are so many neat things Lydia and her family had displayed all over. Why hide these?"

"I have no idea. But, I would say the bigger question is . . . whom did these belong to and why did Grandma have them?"

Mario is busy taking photos. "We should show these to Sam. He might be able to shed some more light on how they all fit together, especially if he can pinpoint some dates for us. That would help in our research. And, Clark may have seen some things like these in his business. He'll be here in the morning."

"I agree. As soon as you are finished taking photos, let's take it all to your place for now. But, first we should look at those paintings downstairs. Millie, will you show us where they are?" Looking over at Millie, she looks like she's seen a ghost.

"Millie, are you okay? What's wrong?"

When we came upstairs, I laid my purse and sketch book on a side table. Millie is staring at the crude drawing I made of the guy in the market who shoved me.

"Millie, what is it?"

"Who is this?"

"It's a drawing I made of a guy who shoved me while we were at the market." I didn't tell her he reminded me of the man in Grandma's hospital room or of the delivery guys. "Why? Do you know him?"

"I need to sit down. I need to think."

Helping her into a chair, I squat down to eye level. "Please take a minute, take a deep breath, and then tell me what you are thinking."

Color is returning to her face as she looks at the drawing once more and then at me. "I don't really know if this is the same man. I just don't know. It could be."

"The same man as who?" Mario puts his hand on Millie's shoulder.

"No. I know it's the same man. The jaw line is the same. So is his mouth. I know it was the same man." Millie is mumbling more to herself than us. She appears to be concentrating.

"Millie. When did you see him and where?"

"When I was coming here I almost ran into him. I apologized even though he actually ran into me. He didn't say anything, but shoved his way past me. He was so rude but I saw him up close. Yes, this is the same man."

"Okay, Millie. This just proves there is some connection with this man and the jewels, music boxes, and what's happening now."

"Why? What's happening now?"

"I don't want to scare you, Millie. But, you should know some people have died and their music boxes stolen. It appears someone or some people want to get their hands on them. We just have no idea why or who for that matter. We want you to be careful and to be safe, Millie."

"Oh dear. What should I do?"

"For now, don't do anything. Just pay attention to people around you. And, don't mention talking to Mario or to me. Okay? Now, let's go downstairs."

Chapter 43

Looking at the first painting, it does indeed have a castle on a hill surrounded by forests. Definitely not the vineyards of my great-grandparents. If you look closely, there is an S on the castle's door. In fact, the door kind of looks like the crest we found up-stairs in the hidden box. They could be from the same family. Still, that doesn't help us know who it belongs to or why the painting is here.

Millie directs us to the dining room to show us the painting of a lady sitting on a terrace overlooking a canal. It's not a large painting, but very detailed. The lady has the tiara on her head, exactly the same as the one upstairs. Looking closer, I notice some-thing else.

"I have that necklace. I have that same necklace. It was in the jewelry box from Grandma."

Moving to look at it, Mario recognizes it. "Yes. It is the same exact one, isn't it?"

Millie moves in to get a better look and says, "That was Lydia's favorite necklace when we would dress up to go to dinner."

"What? You've seen my grandma wearing that necklace? The blue one that changes color in different light?"

"Yes, I have. I even tried it on once. It was the prettiest necklace I have ever seen. My late husband tried to find one just like it for me. This was as close as he could get." Millie shows us a brilliant blue stone on a delicate gold chain around her neck.

I had noticed it when she first showed up but didn't connect the fact that it was similar to the one of Grandma's.

"Okay. That puts a whole different light on the jewelry. Grandma obviously wore it here in Italy. Why did she wait until after she died to give it to me? Why did she keep it hidden all these years?

"And, who is the lady in the painting?"

Millie is staring at the painting. Mario asks her what she sees.

"The balcony in this painting must be from one of the other bedrooms here. Could this be Lydia's mother? Look at her eyes and nose. Doesn't she resemble Lydia? It makes sense that she would have the necklace on that Lydia loved. I don't understand the tiara, though."

"You could be right. Except . . . what other bedroom looks out over this canal? I thought we looked through all the rooms and Grandma's room was the only one looking directly over this canal. Or maybe the artist just used that canal and it wasn't really the scene from that terrace.

"And, I have no idea about the tiara. Were those worn back then?"

Millie looks at her watch and tells us she must leave fairly soon. "I'm having dinner with an old friend and don't want to be late. I could always come back another time. Or, we could see if we can find the balcony where this was painted and then I could leave. The restaurant is only a few minutes from here."

"We don't want to make you late. Why don't you go on ahead? We'll meet here tomorrow to look at the villa more closely. Mario and I must get going as well. I think we've found enough things for one day. We can continue our research online and maybe have more information tomorrow.

"Should we meet you back here about 10 a.m.?"

Chapter 44

Mentally exhausted, Mario and I retired early after a light dinner. More dreams of jewels, royalty, and bad guys filled my head. Still, I awoke rested and ready to start another day of investigation. Brushing my teeth, I sent a glance to Heaven, "Grandma, what did you get yourself into? Give me some clues."

Not getting any immediate help from the Heavens, I headed to breakfast when I heard Clark's voice coming from the terrace. "That was a quick trip. Glad you could come as we have lots to tell you."

"Thanks. Great flight with no delays and I even feel rested. Guess that's what flying first class will do for a long flight."

As we all wake up with coffee, fruit, and pastries, we fill Clark in on our findings yesterday, our meeting with Millie, and her information and memories. All the while he takes notes and looks at the photos Mario took.

"I have seen similar crests, just not this one. They were common in the 1500s to the 1900s to show your family name, your wealth, and your property. The S does make sense, especially with everything pointing to Sante as a name. It's probably the family name, although different renditions could have happened along the way. That wasn't uncommon back then."

"Does the name Sante mean anything to you?"

"No, it doesn't. Have you researched it?"

"Just a little. We were going to do more this morning before we meet Millie at ten o'clock at my villa. We probably don't have time for that and should leave soon, however."

My phone rings and I don't recognize the number. Showing it to Clark and Mario, they tell me to use speaker phone. "Hello."

"You are looking for trouble. Your friend could get hurt. Release all the jewels now and I will leave you alone." The voice is gruff, muffled, and hurried.

"What do you mean? What friend? What jewels?" I'm cut off in mid-sentence and a beep beep is all that's left.

Clark grabs my phone and tries to trace where the call originated. He gets nothing. "Someone knows you're here, knows something about the jewels, and thinks you have a friend. That could mean me, or Mario, or it could mean Millie. Do you have a way to get in touch with her?"

"Oh my goodness. I hadn't thought of Millie getting entangled in all of this mess. No, she didn't give me a cell phone number. Let's get to my villa and see if she is there."

In reality, it only took a few minutes to make it to my front door. It seemed longer. Millie was nowhere to be seen. "Damn. I really hope she's okay. She didn't even tell us where she lives. Why didn't we get more information from her?"

"Let's go inside and show Clark what we've found. Millie will ring the doorbell when she gets here. We are a little early." Mario ushers us all inside after looking up and down the street and locks the door behind us.

Clark had already inspected the inlaid box, tiara, and crest at Mario's so we showed him the paintings in the den and dining room. "I would agree that the crest and the S on the castle are the same family. Many families used their crests in all sorts of places.

"The tiara on the lady in the painting definitely looks like the one you found. I do recognize the necklace, as well. But, you have no idea who this lady is?"

"No. None. Millie thought she looked like Grandma because the nose and mouth are similar. Since Millie knew Grandma at a much younger age than I did, she could be right. But, we have no idea why she would be wearing a tiara and a stunning necklace.

"Oh, I almost forgot. We were going to search through the villa to see if we could find this balcony that overlooks this canal. It's possible it was just the artist's idea, however."

Clark, as an art expert, tells us, "No, I think most artists back then used real scenes. We should see if we can find it. Also, show me where you found the box."

We all head upstairs to Grandma's bedroom suite and Mario takes Clark to the hidden spot in the closet. I keep listening for the doorbell but don't hear anything. Should we be worried?

Chapter 45

We decide to inspect each room more carefully, this time looking for hidden doorways, moving furniture, and sliding rugs. How many times can we look through here, I wonder? But, this time we're looking for things out of the ordinary or that might not make sense.

Searching Grandma's bedroom, we find nothing more than the hidden spot in the closet and the hidden drawer in the night-stand that Millie already showed us. Both of those spots are empty.

Moving on to the sitting room, again we find nothing. Nothing in her bathroom, either. The window overlooks a canal, but not the one in the painting.

We've completed the entire floor and found nothing. "What the heck are we looking for, anyway? The other windows and terraces have lovely views, but not the one from the painting. Grandma wouldn't have covered up a window, would she?" I'm mumbling to myself.

Clark comes alive. "What did you say?"

"Um. I was just wondering if any windows could have been covered up. But, why? And, what are you thinking?"

"You did say this went through a renovation, didn't you?"

"Well, yes. But, I thought that was before they started living here. Do you think the painting was done before the renovation was complete? And, why cover up a perfectly good window?"

"Let's go back to the smaller bedroom at the end of the hall. Something is bothering me about that one."

We're interrupted by the doorbell. It rings and rings and rings . . . three long rings in a row. Looking at each other, we all scramble down the main staircase. Mario gets to the lower level first, unlocks, and yanks open the door. Millie is standing there ready to ring the doorbell again as she collapses into Mario's arms. She's disheveled and out of breath as she looks back over her shoulder.

Mario brings her inside as Clark steps out to survey the street and canal. Seeing nothing, he shuts and locks the door.

Helping her up the first flight of stairs and to a chair in the foyer, Mario kneels down to get a good look at Millie. "What happened? Can you tell me what happened?"

I've grabbed a glass of water and hand it to Millie, who takes a big gulp. "I saw him. He grabbed my arm and tried to steal my handbag. He almost shoved me into the canal. I think he had a friend in a boat. He was the guy. That guy. His eyes are black and he has a really square jaw. He wanted my handbag but I wouldn't give it to him. He told me Lydia was going to die. Isn't she already dead?"

Millie takes another drink and looks around at us. "Did you see him? He said he was at my villa. I don't have a villa."

We aren't sure if Millie is coherent or rambling from fright.

Chapter 46

Once we get Millie calmed down, I gently ask her if she can remember what happened. She nods.

"I was on my way here from the market. I was going to bring fruit and pastries for you. Oh dear, I seemed to have dropped my bags. Where could they be?"

"Millie, that's okay. We'll get them later. Please, go on. You were coming here from the market, right?"

"Yes. Yes, I was. I was so happy to see you and tell you what I remembered after we parted yesterday. I thought we could celebrate. Now, we have nothing to celebrate with. Oh dear."

"We have plenty of food we can use for celebrating. And, remember my family makes the best Prosecco. What's better than that? I'll get us all a glass as soon as we hear a little more about your morning. What did you remember that you wanted to tell us?"

"Ah, yes. Last night I had a dream. Only it wasn't like any other dream. Lydia was standing in my bedroom and she told me she wanted me to remember the painting she once showed me. It's the painting in the bedroom that belonged to her mother. The small bedroom at the end of the hall. She took me there once to show me a secret. I had completely forgotten about it. I guess the tiara threw me for a loop."

"Go on, please."

"Anyway, I only saw Lydia's mother one time. She was in her bedroom, packing to go back to the farm. Lydia's father was already there. That's it. I saw the trunk she was using to pack some things into. Only I think that was the trunk she left here. I have to think about that."

Squeezing her eyes, Millie seems to be either remembering or taking a nap. Not quite sure which.

All of a sudden she continues, "Lydia begged and begged her mother to show us the painting and its magical tricks. I had no idea what she was talking about. Her mother finally agreed but made us both promise not to tell anyone . . . ever. She was so stern and so demanding on this . . . don't ever, ever tell anyone. I must have completely blanked it out of my brain. Silly me. You, Marta, of all people should know about this."

"Millie, I agree I should know. But, what am I to know?"

Clark steps up to Millie. "Can you show us this painting? I think I've already figured out what it is, but I would really like you to show us."

Millie takes Clark's hand as they climb the staircase to Lydia's mother's bedroom. Mario and I exchange glances and follow.

Entering the smallest bedroom, we all see the painting on the side wall that Millie is pointing to. It's rather large for the wall with an ornate heavy frame. "See this painting?"

Looking closely at it, it certainly doesn't look like it would hold any secrets. The Grand Canal of Venice is portrayed, with merchant boats, vaporetti, and gondolas all working their way through the maze. It's well done, but nothing jumps out at me.

Apparently Clark knows what he's looking for as he directs Millie toward the painting.

"Millie, which way do I turn it?"

Mario and I look at him, at the painting, and at Millie.

"Clark, my dear boy, look at the gondola in the center of the painting. Do you see it?"

"I certainly do. I knew something was off but I missed it before. I thought it would turn or move. But, now I see exactly what to do."

Mario is as confused as I. He steps closer to the painting, looking at it carefully. "Clark, what on earth are you talking about?"

"Marta and Mario, look at the gondola in the middle of the Grand Canal. Look closely at the seats. Do you see an ornate seat with a fancy S on the seat back?"

"Yes, I do." We say in unison.

With a confused look, I ask, "So? What does that mean? Other than it's an S like we keep seeing?"

"Watch this. Right, Millie?" Millie nods as Clark runs his finger over the S on the gondola's seat and pushes a slightly raised button that is all but undetectable to a casual observer.

Chapter 47

A soft click, followed by a thunk, and the entire wall disappears quietly into a concealed pocket door panel. We all stand and stare, our mouths hanging open. This small bedroom just gained several hundred more square feet, a gorgeous terrace, an armoire, an old trunk, two brocade covered chairs, and the view of the canal in the painting downstairs.

"What the hell." Mario is the first to speak.

"Why would Grandma's mother or father hide this beautiful part of the bedroom?" Finding my voice, I look at Millie. "Did you actually see this room before?"

"Yes. Just the one time. Then we were forbidden to talk about it, so I forgot about it. Until last night, that is, when Lydia came to me in my dream. I wonder why she wanted me to find it now?"

Looking at Millie again, I had forgotten to ask about her run in with the guy at the market. "Millie, before we look through this room, can you tell us more about the guy who pushed you? We need to see if any of this is connected."

Millie sits down and says, "Let me start at the beginning.

"I told you I was having dinner last night with a friend, right? Well, she kept looking over my shoulder at someone. When I asked her what or who she was looking at, she said a young guy kept glaring at us. She said he was rude. When I turned to look at him, he pulled a hat down over his eyes and left the restaurant. I didn't get a good look at him. We were glad to be rid of him.

"When we were walking home, she lives in the same building as I do, she said she saw him by the doorway. We asked the doorman but he hadn't seen anyone. I forgot about him. Until this morning . . .

"I stopped at my favorite bakery and bought pastries. I picked out special ones. I sure wish I wouldn't have dropped them. I bought the flaky ones with a fresh fruit glaze. They are so good. Do you suppose someone picked up my bag?"

"Millie, I'm sure we can get more. Please continue."

"Right. Anyway, next I stopped at the market to get some cheese and fruit. I was still thinking about the dream and seeing Lydia again that I really wasn't paying any attention to anyone around me. Silly of me, I suppose.

"I had just bought everything I wanted and turned to leave when someone grabbed my arm. It was the arm with all my bags on it and I thought they were trying to steal my bags or even my handbag. When I turned toward him to brush him off, he gave me a huge push toward the canal. I lost my balance, slipped, and dropped my bags. I didn't really fall down. I bumped into something . . . I'm not quite sure what. But, it broke my fall, anyway.

"I tried to regain my balance and I was looking for my bags when he pushed me again. I landed on my knees. I could see another guy in a small boat telling him to hurry up and get me. It was very clear the guy in the boat wanted me in it.

"Something clicked in my brain, apparently. I knew I wasn't going in that boat. I grabbed the first thing I saw and swung it at the feet of the one who pushed me. At the time, I didn't really think about what I was doing. But I must have connected with his feet or ankles or something.

"He yelped, swore, and awkwardly jumped into the boat and they sped off. People were yelling at them by now and someone was helping me up. One man took the iron rod out of my hand, complimenting me on my good aim."

Once again we are all staring at Millie as she relates her story. This woman may be getting up there in years, but not in spunk!

"Millie, that's terrible. We are so glad you made it okay. You mentioned you knew this guy or something. Can you remember what he looked like?" Clark is in his full investigative mode.

Millie shuts her eyes. When she opens them, she asks for my sketch pad. "Let me see if I can draw him first. I have such a clear picture of him in my mind. Then let me see your drawing, Marta."

Chapter 48

Mario came back into the bedroom with a tray, four glasses, and a chilled bottle of Prosecco. "I think we all need to toast the fact that Millie is a quick thinking lady."

Clark and I have finished looking at Millie's sketch and comparing it to the one I drew a few days ago. It definitely could be the same man. We both captured his eyes, square jaw, and mouth in the same way.

Clark excuses himself as he makes a phone call while Mario, Millie, and I drink our Prosecco and look around our new-found room. "Millie, does this room look like you remembered? Or, has it changed? Did Grandma ever give you any explanation of why it was closed off like this?"

Mario sets his glass on the tray and looks out over the canal from the terrace. "This is most certainly the terrace in the painting downstairs. Now, we have the location, the tiara, and the necklace. What we don't have is who the woman in the painting is."

Millie is staring at the trunk. "What is it, Millie? Do you remember something?"

"Remember I told you Lydia's mother had packed away some things in a trunk for her trip to the farm?"

"Yes. Could this be the trunk? I thought it would have been kept at the farm, if indeed she did take it."

"All I remember is Lydia's mother in here, folding clothes, the enameled box on the floor as if ready to be packed, and something else I can't quite put my finger on. I just can't remember what else was here. I do know her mother was not happy to see us."

"Why do you say that?"

"Because she told us we could tell her goodbye downstairs. She told us we needed to forget we even saw this room and not to mention it to anyone. She was very specific about that. We were not to mention this room at all. Ever."

"Did she say why?"

"No. Not that I remember. She looked . . ." Millie pauses as she tilts her head, trying to picture the woman in this room. "She looked sad and at the same time, she looked not well. She was very pale."

"I wonder if she knew she was dying. Grandma didn't really tell me anything about her death or her funeral for that matter. I don't even know where she or my great-grandfather is buried. For all I know, they could have a private cemetery on their property or they could have buried her in the Alps or in . . ."

Millie jumps out of her chair, not letting me finish. "What did you say?"

"I'm sorry. I didn't mean to sound so heartless. I just didn't . . ."

Interrupting me again, "No. Not that. What did you say about the Alps?"

"I was just making a broad statement since I have no idea where they are buried. Why?"

Squeezing her eyes, Millie holds up her hands. "Wait. Something else Lydia's mother said. Something about coming to the Alps to visit her . . . I think she was preparing for a trip to the Alps somewhere. Would that have been possible?"

"But, I still don't know why she was upset with Lydia and me finding her in this room. I guess I'll never know that."

"That's okay. Let's look through the trunk. Maybe it holds some answers. Mario, please help me lift this lid. It's a lot heavier than it looks."

Clark comes back into the bedroom just as we get the heavy lid raised up. Dust filters through the sunlight as we move the top layer of heavy cloth.

"I just scanned both sketches and sent them to Interpol and Scotland Yard. You'll never guess what they told me."

Chapter 49

Mario, Millie, and I are so mesmerized by the trunk and its contents, we don't even hear Clark.

Under the protective layer of cloth is the most spectacular gown I have ever seen. Afraid to pull it out for fear of damaging it, I gingerly touch it. The softest velvet I have ever felt, the light blue gown is adorned with gems that sparkle as the light hits them. Looking at Millie, she's as mesmerized as I am in its beauty.

"Do we dare move it?"

Mario nods his head and helps me gently lift it out. Laying it on the bed, the gown, heavier than it looks, becomes even more spectacular when we can see the whole thing.

"Millie, have you ever seen this before?"

"No. I certainly would have remembered this. I think it matches the necklace in the painting."

"I guess it does. But, why? And, why store it in here in a room that isn't supposed to exist? I don't get it. Is there anything else in the trunk?" I turn and see Clark staring into it. "Clark, what is it?"

"Come here and look. We need to be careful with this. I'm hoping it's what I think it is."

Carefully, Clark lifts out what appears to be a large book with a faded red velvet cover and gold edged pages.

"Clark, what is it? It looks like a family album. But, I don't think they had photos back then, did they?"

"No. I think it is a family registry where they kept family documents. This could answer some of our questions. But, we need to be very careful when we open the pages. They could be so old, they might tear or disintegrate."

Millie is still looking at the gown. "I wonder how old this is. My friend I went to dinner with last night is a seamstress. She worked for a tailor for years and then opened her own business. Now, she's retired . . . sort of. She could probably tell us all about this gown. Should I call her?"

Mario and I look at each other. "Before we involve someone else, what did you say when you came back in the room, Clark?"

"Right. I scanned the sketches, sent them to Interpol and Scotland Yard, and they both called me. It seems you are both quite the sketch artists. This is more than likely the same person. They are also quite certain this is the man who is being sought in several of the murders connected to the music boxes. He is wanted in the US, in Milan, and in London.

"This is where it gets interesting. The name he goes by most of the time is Leo Sante. But, he has other aliases, too. He works for and is probably funded by a ruthless art collector in London by the name of Reid. That's the only name they have . . . Reid. Could be a first name or a last name. They aren't sure yet.

"Anyway, Reid is not a nice guy. He'll kill just to get a piece of art he wants. Doesn't matter if he even keeps it for very long. If he wants it . . . he gets it, whatever the cost. Any way he can. Seems like this Sante guy does a lot of his dirty work. He's not very nice, either. They've got his fingerprints at several of the crime scenes. Now, they want to catch him. They would love to arrest Reid as well."

Mario, Millie, and I are all looking at Clark as he's relaying this information. We're surprised, shocked, and in disbelief.

Clark continues, "So you see, this is serious business. We need to formulate a plan on how to stay safe. The Interpol agents are coming to your villa this afternoon, Mario, to talk to all of us. Millie, you, too. None of us goes anywhere alone for now."

I'm the first to formulate a complete sentence as Mario is shaking his head and Millie just looks lost. "Clark, what do these guys want from us? Did this all start with Grandma's dying and sending me her music boxes and jewelry?"

"We honestly don't know at this point. The music boxes seem to be a focal point and it may be that Reid wants the whole collection. Why now? We don't know. Let's take this registry to Mario's, look through it, and see if we can find anything about your family, Marta."

Mario ushers Millie to a chair before she falls down, "Let's put the gown back and close this room. Then we can lock everything up here and go to my place. Okay?"

"Wait. It's in the armoire. Lydia told me last night in my dream. I just remembered."

"What?" We all ask in unison.

"The armoire." Distinctly and with a nod, Millie says, as if she's talking to complete idiots.

"Okay, what's in the armoire?"

Millie stands up and pulls open the small drawer on the bottom. Mario is closest and removes an ivory colored map. "It's a map of the area where Lydia's parents have their farm and vineyards. I see the towns close by. We'll take it with us and look at it more closely. Let's go to my villa and have lunch. Then we can figure out what to do."

Millie turns to him, "I don't want to burden you. I can go to my own home."

"No." Emphatically, we almost startle Millie.

"Okay. Lead the way. I'm game."

What a delight this woman is.

Chapter 50

Everything put away in my villa, we leave the newly discovered doors to the bedroom open and we all head to Mario's with Clark carrying the registry and Mario carrying the map. Millie seems to be the only one carrying on a conversation as she points out shops and back alleys she wants me to see.

Clark's phone rings startling us all. After a brief conversation, he tells us he'll fill us in as soon as we're at Mario's. He doesn't look happy.

Mario's cook meets us at the door speaking rapid-fire Italian at Mario. They carry on quite the conversation with the cook finally going back to the kitchen and Mario explaining. "Apparently there were two men here trying to deliver a large box of food. Our cook did not order any deliveries and wouldn't let them in. They were very insistent they be let in to unpack the food. He was just as insistent and then they became quite agitated. He said they didn't even look like the delivery men he normally uses. But, what really made him suspicious was the way they talked to each other. One man had an English accent and one was definitely German or Austrian. The Englishman kept telling the other man that somebody wasn't going to be very happy.

It's possible they thought our cook didn't speak anything except Italian and couldn't figure out what they were saying. He never let on he could understand them. As they were leaving, they told him they would be back. This was said to him in Italian. Then they left, still angry at each other.

"This was about an hour ago. Clark, what do you think about this?"

"Well, it seems things are heating up. Somebody is either getting careless or desperate. I need to fill you in on my phone call."

"Agreed. But, let's all go to the terrace for lunch. We can also show the sketches to our cook and see if he recognizes them as either of the men who were here."

As we sit down, I'm trying to take in all the events that have happened since Grandma died. Turning to Clark, "How and why did all this mess start? Did Grandma have any knowledge as to what she had? Do you think I started something when I took the music box and jewelry to have it appraised? Is any of this connected?"

Clark smiles and me and says, "Well, let me tell you about the latest events. The phone call I just received was from my FBI contact in San Francisco. The jeweler you had appraise your things, Marta, has been found. Remember he went missing after his shop was broken into?"

We all relax a little, thinking this is a good turn of events . . . until Clark continues.

"He washed up on shore. His throat was slit and the sharks were unkind to him."

Now we aren't relaxed, but saddened.

"Marta, are you sure neither you nor Lydia ever contacted this man before?"

"Definitely not me. But, I don't really know about Grandma. He wasn't one of her regular Italian buddies she would have lunch or coffee with, that I know of. I don't think he was even Italian and his shop wasn't in North Beach. Why?"

"He had a piece of paper wrapped in plastic, in his inside pocket with Lydia's name and a phone number on it. It's your phone number, Marta."

"What? Why Grandma's name and my number? I don't get it."

"The FBI doesn't know. They're trying to match any handwriting but it's going to be difficult due to the condition of the paper. We need to eat before I finish the rest of the phone call."

In unison, Millie, Mario, and I ask, "Why?"

"Please, just trust me. Let's eat and all have a glass of this excellent Prosecco. Then I will talk."

Chapter 51

You would have thought we had nothing better to do than eat, drink, and chat about Venice as Millie knew it as a little girl. It turns out we learned quite a bit about Millie as she told us tales of following the older bakers and chefs around. Her parents died when she was only six and she lived with an elderly aunt who paid no attention to her. The people at the bakery looked out for her and apparently her aunt didn't care.

That's why she and Grandma were such good friends, despite the age difference.

Lunch finished, the table cleared, and we all had another glass of wine as we looked to Clark.

"I want to finish telling you what I know then I have some questions for all of you. Okay?"

Nodding our heads collectively, Clark proceeds.

"Let me start at the beginning as I know it. That may shed a little light on the whole matter. Then, as Mario suggested, we need to do a timeline. Marta and Millie, you will both be instrumental in placing people and events. Millie, I hope you have nothing pressing for the next several days."

"No. Not really. I have a cat at home that I really should check on. He doesn't like it when I'm gone for long periods of time. He's kind of a big baby. I could go there after we're done listening to you."

"Not alone, you won't. Millie, either Clark or I will go with you and we can bring the cat back here to my villa. I don't think she should go alone, do you Clark?"

"Not at all. Mario has a good idea. After my story is finished you will see why.

"Here's what I know. Sometime between the 1400s and the 1600s a collection of ornate, jeweled music boxes was made for several female members of a ruling family. Originally, it was thought there were ten of these. But, we don't know for sure. We think the family was Austrian or Hungarian. The borders would move a little depending on who was in charge. Or, maybe the rulers moved. At any rate, these were meant to be fancy little boxes to sit on dressers and night stands. They were passed down from generation to generation.

"They gained popularity and value as the decades progressed. Then, for some reason, they all disappeared. No mention of them for years, decades really.

"Fast forward to the 1930s and there is mention of some small gold music boxes covered with gemstones. No idea where they came from, who found them, or who had them all this time. Only a few were discussed. Less than five.

"All of a sudden a couple more surfaced in early 1990, showing up at an auction house. They created quite the buzz in the art world. That's when the murders started. We now know those early murders were directly related to the music boxes. We just don't know why.

"That's kind of the way it is with art thieves. Usually they just steal, not commit multiple murders. This series of thefts and murders is different when this fellow Reid came into the picture. Interpol will fill us in more on him when they get here in an hour.

"I think you and Mario have figured out where Lydia and Luigi got their boxes, Marta. What we need to work on is who knew they had them, both here and in San Francisco, how and when did Lydia get hers to the US, and who knows you have them now, Marta."

Chapter 52

Taking in Clark's story, we all nod. I know I have questions. But, I want to wait for Clark to finish.

"The jeweler from San Francisco that washed up on shore has been identified and he's not a legitimate jeweler. He's a conduit for stolen art. His assistant, Pete, was really working for him trying to negotiate some deals for all sorts of stolen jewelry. He must have thought he hit the jackpot when he saw your music box and jewelry, Marta."

"But, my attorney suggested him as a reputable jeweler to appraise my things. Why would he do that?"

"Probably because the jeweler had a very good cover in place. What better way to find out who has what valuables than to make yourself accessible to attorneys. They send good clients to you with expensive trinkets or jewelry. He was a smart cookie . . . until he wound up dead. He must have crossed the wrong guys.

"Now, Marta I need you think about the times your grandma came to San Francisco to visit you. Who else did she visit, did she go alone, do you have names, and can you think of anything else that would help us? Try to remember as we start our timeline.

"What about Sam? We need to bring him in on what's been happening. Mario, do you want to call him?"

"Will do. I was just thinking about him. He should have some answers for us by now."

"Millie, let's you and I go to your place and bring your cat back here. You can also get anything you might need to stay here for a few days."

"This sounds like fun. But, are you sure it's really necessary? I don't have any music boxes or jewelry."

"Absolutely, it's necessary. Did you forget about the men at the market who wanted you in their boat?"

"Right. Do you really think they were after me?"

Not wanting to upset her, Clark gently takes her arm and says, "Millie, we are dealing with some ugly people who want to get their hands on Marta and Mario's music boxes and jewelry. We don't know why. They don't know that you don't have anything like that. They could just as easily harm you. Let's play it safe for the next few days. Okay?"

Nodding, Millie allows Clark to escort her to her place as Mario comes back from calling Sam.

"He doesn't answer his cell phone or at his shop. That's not like him. I wonder if I should go there."

"Mario, Clark and Millie just left for her place. Maybe we should wait until they return or wait until the guys from Interpol are here. I'm not real sure why they are coming or what we can possibly learn from them. Are you?"

"Not really. I thought it was because that guy, Reid, was involved. But, I don't know anymore."

"Yeah, I know. All I wanted to do is find out where Grandma got the music boxes and the jewelry. Now I wonder about the gown, the hidden room, and oh . . . the map you brought from my villa and the registry Clark had. Where are they?"

"I laid the map on the table when we arrived and found our cook so upset. Let me get it and we can look at it until Clark and Millie get back. Then we'll look through the registry."

Unfolding the old vellum-like paper carefully we see it is a hand drawn map of plots of land. There is a large crown on one of the larger pieces, some writing neither of us can decipher on other parts, and an S on several other parts of land. If this is a real map, it appears to show ownership.

"Mario, look at the S. It's written the same as all the other ones. Do you suppose that land belongs to the family with the S? Could it somehow be related to Grandma or her mother?"

Turning over the paper Mario gets a puzzled look on his face. "What is it?"

"Marta, look. I think what we have is a deed. I have no idea if it's official or even where this land is. But, it has a date, signatures, and a royal seal. At least it says it's a royal seal. Maybe we should take this to our attorney to see what it is. Lydia used the same attorney's firm as I do. The firm is reliable and would have resources to explain this.

"I'm going to call and see if we can visit with my attorney later today. Then we can stop by Sam's and see what he's found out about your jewelry. Maybe by then we'll have more information from Interpol and know what we're doing and why."

"I would certainly like that, Mario. I sure wish I could talk to Grandma. I'm going to put this map and the registry away until Clark returns."

Chapter 53

Mario and I are in the dining room with the two men from Interpol. We've cleared out everything from Grandma and Luigi. Clark and Millie have not yet arrived from her place and we're a little worried until I receive a text from Clark telling us they're on their way.

Bill and Thomas, from Interpol, want to wait for Clark and Millie so the four of us sit stiffly sipping our coffee. They're pleasant yet reserved and I can tell small talk is not their forte. Thankfully, Clark, Millie, and her cat arrive before any of us feel any more uncomfortable.

Nervously playing with her hands, Millie starts to speak until she sees Bill and Thomas. Looking at Clark, he whispers something to her and she puts her cat in his carrier down and opens the latch. Tiger ambles out, looks at us as if to say he has new servants and lies down on the rug to groom his paws. Millie looks worried but takes a seat at the dining room table next to me.

"Are you okay, Millie?" I whisper to her.

"I don't know. Clark told me to wait. I'll tell you later."

Clark greets the two men, introduces himself and Millie, and tells them we would all like to hear what they have to say. Looking at Millie, I can tell they wonder how she is involved but they proceed anyway.

Thomas takes notes while Bill speaks. "Clark, you know some of the story, but let me fill you all in on more events of the last couple of months. I would like you all to listen before you ask questions.

"Most of this revolves around the music boxes like those you have in your possession. A man, by the name of Reid, wanted by the FBI for art theft in the United States moved to London a few years ago. Scotland Yard and our agency became involved when he not only stole valuable art but was tied to several murders. Some of the thefts and murders were connected to the music boxes, among other things.

"We aren't sure how or why he decided he wanted these, but he seems determined to acquire the entire collection. You already know about the murders in San Francisco, San Diego, Milan, and London. All with the same modus operandi, or M.O. for short, most with his same associates doing the dirty work.

"It appears he has no legal or real connection to any of the music boxes; he just wants them and wants them immediately if not sooner. He doesn't care who is in his way or how he gets them. He probably has no intention of selling them but that doesn't make them any less valuable to him. He doesn't need the money.

"Marta, we don't know how your grandmother acquired hers. We do know she mentioned them to several people in San Francisco a few years ago, as one the men she talked to also had one. He was a former San Francisco private investigator turned art collector . . . a legitimate art collector who researched what she had shown him to see if it matched his. We found out recently that Pete worked at his shop for a brief time. I don't know if you ever went to his shop with your grandmother. His name was Enrico and his shop was called Enrico's Art For Life."

Nodding, I decide to hold my comments and questions until he finishes.

"This might have been the start of Reid's discovery. You see, Pete and Mr. Johnson, who you contacted, were employees of sorts of Reid. We think they had been working for Reid for years. As maybe Clark has told you, Pete and Mr. Johnson are both dead. As for Enrico, he was the first murdered.

"About a year before your grandmother died, Enrico confronted Pete at his shop. Looking at the shop's surveillance tape, he discovered Pete was attempting to open the safe where Enrico kept his music box. When he entered one night to catch Pete in the act, Pete tortured and then brutally murdered Enrico, destroyed the shop to look like a robbery gone bad, and managed to open the safe. He probably got the combination out of Enrico before killing him.

"I know you have questions. Please let me continue. Then you came into Mr. Johnson's shop. We're sure he couldn't believe his eyes when he saw your music box. Following that, the rest of the murders have occurred and several music boxes have been stolen. We don't know how many Reid has or how many more exist. We know of your music box, Marta. Do you know of any more?"

Mario and I exchange glances, then we look at Clark.

Clark tells them there are several more, he relates a few stories that go along with them, and tells them we will fill them in once they finish telling us why they came here.

"Fair enough. I'll continue. Then you can tell us about those.

"The sketches of the two men Clark sent to me match the ones we have from grainy surveillance tapes and other witnesses. They appear to be working for Reid, trying to acquire the music boxes. However, there is a new development in that area.

"One of the men is dead. Venice police found him floating in a canal about an hour before we arrived here. His throat was slit.

"The thing that confuses the Venice police is what he had in his pocket.

"He had two photos. One of Marta and one of Millie. They were taken yesterday at your villa, Marta."

Chapter 54

A collective gasp fills the dining room. Then confusion, as we all try to speak at once.

Holding up his hand, Bill says, "Wait a minute, please. This is disturbing to you, I know."

"No kidding." I want to say something more cutting but try to restrain myself. "What does this mean for Millie and for me? What do we do, Clark?"

Bill looks at Millie and then at Clark and asks, "You seem to have some more information. You and Millie were at her home, right? Did you find something?"

Millie can hardly contain herself. "You bet we did. Tell them, Clark."

"When we arrived, Millie first noticed her flower pot by the front step was missing. Then, when we went up to the first floor, she noticed it sitting by the door." Millie nods her head in agreement.

"We cautiously entered and Millie immediately saw several things that were misplaced."

Millie jumps up and says, "Tiger did not coming running to greet me. He's more like a big puppy than a cat and always greets me. He was hiding under the bed. That's not like him."

Clark continues, "When we went into the bedroom we discovered someone had rummaged through Millie's jewelry box. She doesn't think anything was taken but it was a mess. That's when Tiger came out of hiding.

"We looked around some more, Millie packed a bag, put Tiger in his carrier, and headed out the door. That's when things became a little confusing until you just told your story. You're going to want what we found.

"Millie picked up the flower pot to move it back downstairs by the front door when she found this." Clark pulls a plastic bag out of his pocket containing a knife with dirt and something red stuck to it.

Once more we utter a collective gasp. He hands the bag to Thomas and Bill.

Thomas gets on his phone as Bill takes some photos of it. "This is most likely the murder weapon that killed the man in the canal. Someone probably thought it would be a long time before Millie searched her flower pot. I sure hope we can get some prints off it. That would give us a break we desperately need.

"I think it's time to hear everything all of you have or know. Clark, why don't you go first and tell us what you know? Then, Marta and Mario can fill in the blanks. Millie, I need you to pay close attention to their stories to fill in any past history that could possibly be useful."

Clark tells them what he knows about the music boxes, Mario fills in a couple of spots about Grandma and Luigi finding them, Millie adds her recollections, and I relate the events that happened starting with Grandma's warnings, the guy in the hospital, and ending with coming here. Since this isn't about the jewelry and since Clark didn't bring that up, I don't mention it, either.

Bill is nodding and Thomas is taking notes, but looks up when we mention additional music boxes. "You mean you have more music boxes? Where are they?"

Mario speaks, "Yes. We have four more here in my safe. Two belong to Marta and two are mine. Do you want to see them?"

Nodding, Bill says, "Clark, I assume you have looked at them and can tell us if they are genuine and are part of the collection."

"I have and to the best of my knowledge of this collection, they are a part of it. I'm not sure how many Reid has or if there really were 10 or even as many as 12. I've read and heard different numbers. I have never heard that they have been copied, however."

Mario brings them to the dining room table. Sitting there together, they are stunning. I can't imagine seeing all 10 in one spot. No wonder Reid wants them all. They would make a spectacular sight.

Putting on gloves, Bill and Thomas inspect all four. "I agree, Clark. These appear to be from the same collection as the ones we've seen. We need to check how many have been stolen and if there is any other chatter about this type of art. For now, is your safe secure enough, Mario?"

"It's been here since this villa was a palace. I've had it inspected as I keep many important items and documents in it. I do believe it would take dynamite to open it. An accomplished safe cracker could probably also open it, but it would take a while."

"Good. Let's leave them there for now."

Something dawns on me. "What is Reid going to do next to get his hands on these? He already had someone take photos of Millie and me. It seems like it's just a matter of time before someone else gets killed or we are harmed. As much as I don't want to lose Grandma's music boxes, should we just contact him and offer to sell them to him?"

Everyone is looking at me like I have just suggested we all fly to the moon. Clark is the first to respond. "Absolutely not. He doesn't want to buy anything he goes after. For guys like him, stealing is the ultimate challenge. The more difficult, the better. If people get in the way, they're killed. If they resist, they're tortured and then killed. He doesn't care at all about anything but his current challenge. And, that's taking these music boxes from all that have them.

"We need to find him somehow and put an end to this craziness."

Nodding in agreement Bill picks up where Clark left off. "Clark is right. This is a game to Reid. A sick game. He's already killed or had someone kill at least one of his top flunkies. I can't believe he would kill. He's more of a hire it done type of guy. No need to get his hands dirty. So, that makes our work easier and yet harder. Easier, because now we have one less guy to watch for. Harder, because we don't know if he hired another one.

"What we want now is to keep all of you safe. A security detail will be here within the hour to guard all of you for the next few days. As fast as this is moving, things should happen quickly. Reid now knows you have at least one music box, Marta. I have no idea if he knows about the rest."

"Does that mean we are to stay put? We were going to take a trip to my family's vineyards. Can we still do that?"

"That might be a good idea. I suggest Clark and Millie leave here first and then Mario and Marta. You can all meet at the train station. We'll have both of you followed just to make sure everything is okay and we'll have an officer stay here at your villa and one at yours, Marta. Will that work?"

Thomas speaks up, "I should stay here. That way we don't have to inform anyone else about these music boxes."

Bill disagrees. "Thomas, we need to have regular security detail here. You will be needed elsewhere."

"No. I don't think that's a good idea. I will stay here."

Apparently Bill isn't going to argue.

Clark turns to Millie. "Millie, you don't have to go with us. We don't want to put you in any more danger than we already have."

"Why, I absolutely want to go along. I want to see where Lydia grew up and I'm having a great time. It's not every day things like this happen to me. I won't live forever. Danger can find me anywhere. Let's go."

Chapter 55

After we get our act together, pack for a short trip, and meet at the train station we settle in to our seats for the two hours or less ride. Mario has arranged for a car to pick us up once we get to Conegliano. I left a message for my contact, Lorenzo, at the vineyard apologizing for the short notice. Supposedly, he and I co-own the vineyards or the brand or something along that line. I haven't had time to sort that out yet. I'm not even really sure who he is. Is he going to be glad to see me? Or, is this an intrusion?

I guess we'll know by tomorrow. After driving from Conegliano to Valdobbiadene, we'll stay there tonight and I'll contact Lorenzo again before we drive to the property. It's not far, but I don't want to assume it's okay to stay with him.

As the train gets underway, we are offered Prosecco and a snack. With the countryside whizzing by, Clark takes the registry we found in my villa out of his pack. We all gather around the table as he gently opens the cover. Expecting to see old photos, the first page is more like a listing of legal documents.

Clark tells us what he thinks the first page says. "From what I can gather, property deeds are on pages one through ten, birth records are on pages 11 through 15, and family documents are on pages 16 through 25. No mention of whom this belonged to, however. No mention of any names that I can decipher, either."

The pages are quite thick, probably velum, and starting to crumble around the gold edges. Otherwise, it's in remarkable condition. The handwriting is legible and ornate at the same time.

"Well, are we ready for what this might tell us?"

"Yes." In unison, we are all anxious to find out what we have.

Turning the page, we again gasp in unison.

A crest, identical to the ones we have on the door and in jewelry form, covers the entire page. In the middle is a distinctive, large S. Under the crest, at the bottom of the page, are the words Sante Familie.

Looking at all of us, Clark says, "Well, it appears we might have an official book for the Sante family. Considering it was in your grandmother's villa, Marta, it appears this might have been her last name. By the way, what was her name before she married your grandfather? Do you know?"

"Yes. It was Rizzo. I've never heard the name Sante before all this started."

"So, maybe it was her mother's maiden name. That would have been your great-grandmother's name. But why keep it hidden? I wonder about the significance of it. It sort of sounds Italian."

Running his finger gently over the crest, Mario notices it is slightly embossed. "This is fine workmanship in this registry. My guess is, the family was wealthy. Not everyone could afford to have something like this. Do we have a year anywhere on it?"

"Not that I can see. Maybe it will show up later. Did they put years on registries or books like this?"

"I have no idea. Let's keep looking. Clark, will you please do the honors?"

"Sure." As Clark turns to page one, we all see that indeed it is a property deed. "I'm guessing but I think this is written in some sort of legalese German. My German is weak, at best. How about you, Mario? Can you read German?"

"No. I'm sorry. The only German I can really understand or read is when I want to order a beer."

We all laugh as Clark is turning the next couple of pages. Looking like the first one, they appear to be deeds or legal descriptions, as well.

Millie is looking intently at one of the pages. "I can read some German. My late husband and I traveled to Germany quite a bit and I took some language courses. I think this one refers to an estate and a castle. See the words schloss? It appears it includes 250 hectares, or roughly 600 acres."

Now, we're all staring at Millie. This woman is amazing.

Looking up from the registry she says, "What?"

Chapter 56

Clark seems able to speak first. "Millie, that's wonderful. Let's look through these other deeds and see if something jumps out at you."

"Okay. But I don't know much about property deeds. I may be able to pick up only a few words."

"That's okay."

Slowly looking through the remaining pages of deeds, nothing really grabs Millie's attention. I can tell Clark was hoping for something more. I know I was. Mario had stepped away to make a phone call and is now back with us.

"I just talked to our driver. He speaks fluent German. He'll be glad to translate these for us."

"Wonderful. Let's see if the birth records tell us anything we can read."

Turning to page 11, we see these do appear to be records of births. Names we don't recognize, words we can't quite make out, and years that seem to be everywhere from the 1600s to the 1800s. It's obvious we need these translated as well.

"Millie, do any of these make sense?"

"Not any more than you can read. You see the dates and names?"

"I do. Marta, do you have any idea of names your grandmother may have mentioned?"

"No, Clark. I don't. I don't even know what her mother's name or father's names were. That's kind of sad, isn't it?"

"How about you, Mario? Any names you heard your grandfather mention? Or, your parents?"

"Not really. My parents both died within the last year. Mother had cancer and I just don't think my father wanted to live after she was gone. He kind of wasted away. I sure wish I had talked to him more about all of this. He and Grandpa were close. He might have known something. But, it's too late now."

"That's okay. It almost appears as if these are only first names. If indeed this is a book about the Sante family, I guess that would make sense. This could be just a record of who was born when. Not sure. Let's look at the last pages labeled Family Documents. Maybe they will tell us something."

Turning to those pages, Clark angles the registry for Millie so she can get a good look. Pointing to some words and phrases, Millie nods her head.

"I think this page is talking about a ruling family or a royal family. These are the words I think I can decipher. Konigliche means royal; Kohig means king; Konigin means queen; Hohes Gericht means your honor; ehrbar means honorable; die Adelige means lady. I think. I could be off on some spellings or exact meanings, though."

"That's at least a good start. Thanks, Millie.

"It appears we are dealing with some type of royalty, even though it may not be the exact king of somewhere. It could have been king of a small area. History can be so confusing. The real question remains . . . why was this particular book in your grandmother's villa, Marta?"

"I wondered the same thing. I also wonder why it's in German and not in Italian."

Mario nods his head. "Good questions."

Chapter 57

We don't have time to ponder the registry any more as we are at our stop. Marcus, the driver from the company Mario hired, is waiting for us. He greets Mario and introduces himself to the rest of us.

"I am so glad you could come to our part of Italy. And, I am so glad to meet the owner of one of the best Prosecco brands in the whole world." He kisses me on both cheeks. "I love your Prosecco. In fact, I have some chilled and we will drink when we arrive at your hotel. It's not far."

His charm is contagious as he treats us all as his new best friends.

"Mario mentioned you have some German you would like translated. I speak five languages. Well, really I only speak three. But, I can read five. I should be able to help you. What do you need translated?"

Mario is sitting in the front of Marcus' van. "Marta has a registry that has possibly been passed down through her family. We aren't sure. We found it in her grandmother's villa, hidden away. It appears to have deeds, family records, and such. Millie was able to help with some of it and we'd like to know more about what it contains."

Marcus turns to me. "Do you know anything about your family or their history? Do you know if they had important land or pieces of art? Were they wealthy? Did your family have other items of importance, like jewelry or gemstones? Maybe your book is really a clue, is that it?"

"No, I don't. I really only knew my grandma or thought I knew her. Now, I'm finding out all sorts of stories about her and Luigi. When Grandma died a few months ago she left me her cookbooks, some jewelry, and other things. She also mentioned the vineyards, telling me I was a co-owner. Her attorney in Venice has all the paperwork, but I have no idea what I inherited. We all thought it would be a good idea to visit." Since I don't really know how much to tell Marcus, I leave out a lot of details.

I glance at Clark, who is sitting in the back and he nods. Apparently, that was enough to tell him.

"Wonderful. You will find this part of Italy enchanting, enticing, and a producer of the best sparkling wines in the world." Marcus grins and points out landmarks, monasteries, castles, vineyards, taverns, gardens, and more as we make our way through villages and countryside.

It's beautiful country, nestled in the shadows of the Dolomites. Vines wind their way up the steep slopes and small villages are tucked around every corner of this narrow road. We stop to let large trucks pass by and to check out whatever Marcus is pointing to as we continue our journey.

Arriving at a hotel, we all check in and Marcus says he can look at my book while we get settled. When Clark doesn't answer him, he then tells us to meet him in the lobby bar with whatever we want translated. Clark has the registry in his bag and asks if I want to carry it as we make our way to the third floor. Millie and Mario's rooms are on the second floor.

"Not really. I would like you to watch Marcus' face when he translates, however. I want to be sure we're getting the correct translation. I don't know why, but something bothers me about him. I can't put my finger on it. Mario seems to know him, so it's probably just my woman's intuition kicking in from all that's happened." I shrug my shoulders.

"No, Marta, you have good instincts. There is something off about him. I've already scanned a photo of him and sent it to my contact at the FBI. They will work with Interpol, etc. to see if he checks out. For now, let's be careful what we say to him. Okay?"

"Thanks. That makes me feel better. As soon as I've freshened up, let's see what he has to say."

Mario, Clark, and I all arrive downstairs about the same time. Millie is already there and chatting with Marcus. They seem to be getting along. When Marcus sees us, he pours Prosecco for everyone and holds up his glass to make a toast.

"Here's to good friends and to finding out more about secrets and jewelry from Marta's grandmother."

Mario, Clark, and I almost drop our glasses.

Chapter 58

Clark is quickest to react. "What did you say, Marcus?"

"Millie here was just telling me you've had quite the last few days finding hidden jewelry and secret rooms. Lots of action. Now, you have a special book that talks about royalty. I can't wait to find out what this is all about."

Mario picks up where Clark left off. "Marcus, we haven't exactly found anything hidden. Some renovation was done on Marta's villa and a room was redesigned. The book we found is just that, a book. We only brought it because we originally thought it might have maps to Marta's vineyards. Now, we just think it's an old book. It happens to be written in German and we have most of it deciphered. We were hoping you could confirm what we know."

Wow. Mario is a quick thinker. But, I am glad he referred to the registry as just a book. Marcus looks doubtful. Apparently he and Millie had quite the conversation while we were upstairs. It didn't dawn on me to tell her not to say anything to Marcus. And, how did he get so much information out of her in such a short time anyway?

Marcus is not to be deterred. "Why don't you let me see the book and I'll read what I can. Then we'll all know what it's about. If you brought any of the jewelry, I could look at that, too. Jewelry is a hobby of mine."

Thinking Clark had brought the registry downstairs, I look at him questioningly. He looks at Marcus. "I left it in my room by mistake. I was so intent on getting a glass of wonderful Prosecco, I just forgot."

That's funny. Clark doesn't forget anything.

He continues. "Why don't we all take some time and get ready for dinner? It's been a long day and I think we're all ready for dinner. Marcus, please join us and we can show the book to you then."

Marcus is obviously upset at this. "Thank you, but I can't. I have another appointment I need to attend to. Maybe you could bring it to me later tonight."

"I'm sure it will be an early night for us all. Perhaps we can meet you for breakfast. Are you driving us out to see Marta's vineyard?"

"No, I'm not. I have to be out of town for a few days. Another driver will assist you. He will meet you in the morning. I am quite upset I cannot be of service to you with this mysterious book."

"There's no mystery about the book, Marcus. We just thought you could confirm what we already know." Mario is firm but cordial . . . just barely.

"I'm sorry to have lost out on an opportunity to see your book. Now, I must get going. Have a nice evening." It's obvious to all of us, including Millie, Marcus is just barely holding in his anger. What an about face in his demeanor.

As Marcus exits the hotel, we hear his car start, and tires throwing gravel in his apparent haste to leave. Millie stands. "I am so sorry. I feel this is all my fault. He kept asking me questions, almost like he already knew the answers. I figured he must know something so I just filled in the gaps. I shouldn't have said anything, should I?"

I stand and pat Millie's arm. "Don't worry about it. Clark and I had some concerns about him but didn't have time to tell you. Clark didn't bring the registry from his room, so Marcus didn't have a chance to look at it. It's okay, Millie. Really, it is."

"Well, that's not entirely true. I did bring it with me. I just left it on the bench over here when I walked in and saw him trying to cozy up to Millie. I figured something was up. Looks like I was right."

Clark's phone vibrates and he looks at the text he just received. "Well, I'll be. How well do you know him, Mario?"

"I don't know him. The company he works for had done some driving for me in the past and they recommended him. Why?"

"I just received information from my FBI buddies. He's a known associate of Reid. In fact, they're after him for questioning in the murders in Germany."

"Germany?" We all echo. "What murders in Germany?"

Chapter 59

"Let's go in to dinner and I'll fill you in on the texts I received while we were driving here."

Once dinner is ordered and our wine served, Clark tells us what he just found out. "Over the last week two more art dealers were found murdered. These were legitimate art dealers; one with a very high end, exclusive shop and one was more of a collector but would buy and sell from time to time. Both stellar individuals. Both lived in Berlin and probably knew of each other.

"You already can guess what was taken from the first dealer . . . a music box. He was killed at his shop, which was odd. This isn't a shop anyone can walk into. It's in a restricted building with tight security and you have to make an appointment to even enter. He would check out prospective clients before allowing them to make that appointment. That tells Interpol whoever killed him must have either had the credentials or a really good cover in place. They're working on that one.

"The second one, the collector, was attacked at his home. His security was state of the art as well and sent a silent alarm to the police when his attacker broke in. His Doberman took a bite out of the leg of the attacker but not before he shot the dog's owner. His wife walked in just as the police were searching the home. She says nothing is missing. When they showed her photos of the music boxes, she said he had nothing like those. That in itself is odd. Someone must have had wrong information."

We've been listening and eating. Putting down my fork, I ask "Why are they looking for Marcus, though?"

"Even though his face was covered and he wore gloves, the images from the first murder scene matched the images from the second. You see, when the dog bit him he yanked off his mask to try and shoot the dog. The camera didn't get a good look at his face as he kept it down. Then the dog ran out, and the killer didn't waste any time in leaving, too.

"Since these were the same night, the clothing appeared to be the same, the size and shape of the killer was the same . . . they figure it's the same guy.

"Guess what? They're pretty sure it's someone they know who associates with Marcus in his other full time job. This driving job must have been just a way to see what you two have."

"What's his full time job? I would have never guessed he wasn't a regular driver. He seemed to know all about the countryside."

"Scotland Yard and Interpol have him on their radar as an art dealer in London. Surveillance has him coming and going to Reid's estate."

Mario asks, "If they know where Reid lives, why don't they just go in and arrest him?"

"I'm sure they would like nothing better than to do that. However, his estate is heavily guarded and they have no probable cause to just walk in. What I would like to do, Mario, is talk to the driving company you used. We need to see how they happened to hire Marcus for this job."

"Sure. That's a good idea. I've been wondering about that as well. I'll go call them right now. They answer the phone 24/7."

We continue eating and Mario makes his way back into the dining room from outside. "Guess what? They have never hired Marcus before today. He showed up and said a close friend was going to need a driver and he would like to volunteer for the job. He gave them my name and even knew where we were coming from and when. How can that be? Who knew we were coming? Just us and the two guys from Interpol. Right?" He looks at Clark, Millie, and me.

Clark is puzzled and angry. Picking up his cell phone he punches in some numbers. He's not a happy person right now. Millie has caught on to everything being said. She's not just some little old lady without a clue. "At least this time I didn't do anything wrong. The only one I told was Tiger and the last I knew he couldn't really talk. He just listens. I don't understand."

Mario and I smile at her. "No, Millie, it's not you. Marta and I are just as confused as you are right now."

Clark hangs up, looks at us, and says, "There is a problem. A big problem."

Chapter 60

"Let's all go upstairs to my room. I'll fill you all in there. Even though there aren't many people here in the dining room, I just want to be careful. Okay?"

Nodding in agreement, we follow Clark to the third floor. Since there is no lift in this hotel, we walk slowly as to not have Millie overdo it. Clark reaches his room first and notices his door is slightly ajar.

"Wait here, away from the door." Firmly, he instructs us as he pulls out a weapon. Cautiously, he opens the door and flips on the light. That's about all we can see from our spot in the hallway.

Even though it seems likes hours, I'm sure it's only been a couple of minutes before he comes back into the hall, no longer carrying his weapon.

"Apparently we have more problems. Although I can be fairly certain I know who did this." Motioning us to come into his room, we notice clothes thrown all over, dresser drawers opened, his suitcase turned upside down, and the bed completely unmade with covers and sheets stripped off.

"Clark, it's a mess." Millie states the obvious.

"Yeah. I should learn to clean up after myself, huh?"

"Really, though, what happened and who do you think did this?" Mario is just as concerned as the rest of us.

"These are my thoughts. Marcus couldn't get his hands on Marta's registry, even though he desperately and repeatedly tried. Since we know he isn't a real driver, he was here for only one purpose and he couldn't accomplish that. At first.

"If you remember, I told him I had left the book in my room. In reality, I didn't. But, he didn't know that. I think he made a huge effort to leave with a lot of noise so we would think he was gone. Then, when he knew we would be at dinner, he came here hoping to steal it from my room. Only, he couldn't find it.

"What I'm also thinking is that since he couldn't find it here, he probably searched other rooms as well. Marta, yours would be the obvious choice. We need to check your room and then I need to contact someone I trust at Interpol."

"Okay. I'm right across the hall. I didn't notice my door being open, though. Let's look." I start to leave Clark's room and he grabs me.

"Stay here. All of you. Let me check the room. May I have your key?"

A couple of minutes later Clark comes back across the hall and tells me to take a look. He wants to make sure nothing is missing. Looking around my messed up room, I search through my suitcase. At least, I look through what's left of it. It has been completely destroyed, ripped to shreds.

"I really didn't bring anything of any importance with me, Clark. You have the registry and that's really what we are focusing on right now. Why would he do this?"

"My guess is that he's sending a message. He's telling us not to mess with him.

"But what bothers me more is back to the fact that he knew we were going to be here. You're all sure you told absolutely no one about this trip?" Clark looks intently at all three of us.

"No one." We all have the same response.

Millie is picking up sheets and clothes. "Shouldn't we tell the hotel? They could come help us clean up."

"Not yet, Millie. But thanks for thinking of that.

"Okay, this is what I found out on the drive here. A few months ago the FBI and Scotland Yard had a joint effort on a case. At the last minute, an Interpol agent was assigned to help. It was Thomas."

"You mean Thomas as in the Thomas that was interviewing us?"

"Yes, that one. Anyway, the whole operation fell apart when the people they were closing in on disappeared. It was like they knew the authorities were getting close. At the time, someone suspected an insider leaking information. Everything pointed to Thomas, due to some odd conversations. But, no one could prove it.

"Thomas has been watched closely since then and nothing has led anyone to suspect anything out of the ordinary. Maybe he knew he was being watched. Who knows? When he volunteered to help Bill with interviewing you and hopefully finding Reid, he was given the job. He was already in Milan so it was easy for him to come to Venice. No red flags were raised.

"Until . . ." Clark pauses, looks down, and takes a deep breath.

We can tell he's concerned about something. Putting my hand on his shoulder, I ask him, "What is it? What happened?"

"Millie, I want to know if you can handle bad news. Really bad news."

Millie nods. "I'm stronger than I look. I just hope it's not about Tiger."

"No, Tiger is okay. Mario's cook loves him and is taking care of him. It's Bill.

"Mario, your cook found Bill with his throat slit. He was sitting in your dining room, tied to a chair. Your cook had my card and one I gave him from my friend in the FBI. Even though they don't have jurisdiction, I figured he could somehow help. Your cook contacted the FBI and the local Venice police. You have investigators swarming through your villa.

"Your staff is cleaning up the mess with the approval of the authorities. Mario, I'm sorry. I should have picked up on something Thomas said a lot earlier."

Chapter 61

"Clark, what did he say? Is it something we told him or we showed him?" Mario glances at me.

"No. It just bothered me that an Interpol agent would be so insistent on pulling duty hanging around your villa, Mario. That's just not done. Local police and other security men do that. Not Interpol.

"Now, we know why. He was hoping either to find something or break into your safe, Mario. He may have even made a visit to your villa, Marta. But, since Bill was murdered the way he was, he must have been suspicious of Thomas as well. He may have tried to confront him or may have walked in on him doing something."

"Where is Thomas now?"

"They aren't sure. But a man matching his description boarded a train tonight for here. We need to all stick together for a few more hours. Tomorrow some agents I can trust will meet us at your vineyard, Marta. Did Lorenzo ever get back to you?"

"He left me a text. In all the confusion, I forgot. We are to meet him tomorrow morning at ten o'clock. I guess we need a driver, huh?"

"Well, the one I hired last time didn't work out so well. Let me contact the company again and request a regular driver this time. Hopefully, we'll have better luck."

"Okay. I'm going to go downstairs and fill the hotel owner in on our messes up here. I will also get us one new room with two beds. Marta, you and Millie can have the beds. Mario and I will take turns staying awake."

Knowing Clark had valid reasons for this, we didn't argue with him. I didn't really think any of us would get a good night's sleep anyway. I was wrong. Millie snored like a grizzly bear in hibernation. Oh well, at least she slept.

Morning came quickly, although three of us didn't really sleep.

Over morning breakfast of pastries and coffee, Millie hoped we all had a good night. Nodding, we didn't have the heart to tell her she kept us awake half the night with her snoring.

Another text from Lorenzo, giving directions, and then we were off to see my vineyards. My vineyards. Some of these gorgeous looking fields actually belong to me. I couldn't believe it.

This driver wasn't talkative like Marcus but delivered us to a vine covered, stone building with a carved wooden door. Standing in the doorway was a man who looked like he spent plenty of time out in the sun. Removing his hat, he greeted us all profusely in Italian, kissing Millie's and my cheeks, shaking hands, and smiling. Mario said something to him in Italian and he immediately switched to English. I really need to learn Italian.

"Welcome to our winery. I'm Lorenzo and you must be Marta. I didn't know your grandma, but my grandpa knew her. They shared a love of great Prosecco and of beautiful land. I have so much to tell and show you, but first we drink. Come. Come this way." Leading us all into the winery and up a few old wooden stairs we make our way into a beautiful yet simple room. One long table looks like it could have been carved from a single tree, rustic looking yet smooth with years of wear.

A simple silver tray sits at one end with five glasses and an unopened bottle of Prosecco.

"Have you tasted our wines?" Lorenzo looks at me.

"I found some in my grandma's villa in Venice. Prior to that, no. It's delightful the way it dances in my mouth. And, it's not sweet like some I've tasted. I need to learn more from you, though."

Lorenzo looks pleased as he opens the bottle in front of him.

"We'll toast your arrival here and then you can tell me how your trip was."

Raising his glass, Lorenzo taps each of ours. "Cincin."

Chapter 62

Lorenzo exchanges more pleasantries with all of us, charming Millie in the process. Once we've had a tour of the winery, he leads us to another building where he informs us we will have lunch.

"Then I want to know everything. I think there are some things you are not telling me. Okay?"

I'm thinking to myself that Lorenzo must be psychic or something. How does he know what we are or are not telling him? Looking over at Clark, he smiles at me. Then he motions me to a corner of the fabulous dining room with its high ceilings, warm wooden beams, dark polished table, and snow white china arranged precisely on an ivory table cloth. The setting is picture perfect.

"What? What is it about Lorenzo? I know you are thinking something. I can tell it."

Clark nods. "He's not just a wine maker, I'd bet on it. There's a high strung, steely quality about him and his movements. He doesn't miss a thing. He smiles, but not really. He's listening to us even now I'd venture to say."

We move to the table when a woman in chef's whites enters the room and greets us. "Welcome to our home. I am the chef and a good friend of Lorenzo. Now I am a good friend of you. Let me explain the menu for today's lunch."

As we're dining on our wonderful courses of local fare, each accompanied by wines from either Lorenzo or the region, Lorenzo is giving us a history lesson about the area. "When we have dessert I will tell you about your family, Marta. In the meantime, Clark, I believe you have questions about me."

Looking at me, Clark smiles at Lorenzo. "Are you a lip reader or a mind reader?"

Laughing, Lorenzo says, "Neither. I can tell you are wondering about many things. Where would you like me to start?"

"Well, I can't quite put my finger on it but you remind me of someone. Do you want to let us know what you do other than making fabulous wines?" Clark gives nothing away in his remarks. It's sort of like a game of cat and mouse. Only, I don't know who the cat is.

"Let me ask you a question first and then I will tell you my background. Okay?"

"Please, go ahead."

"Clark, you are not just a friend of Marta, Millie, and Mario, are you? You haven't stopped gathering information in your brain since you arrived at the winery."

"Fair enough. You asked. I am a friend but also an investigator of stolen art. I have an extensive background in police work and am working with Marta and Mario to find out more about some items their grandparents left to them. Anything more you'd like to know?"

"Yes. Which branch of your armed forces did you get your training?"

That question startles all of us, including Clark, who chuckles. "I see you are very observant, Lorenzo. In fact, I was indeed, wondering the same thing about you."

Now he has our complete attention. What's the deal?

Laughing, Lorenzo raises his glass to Clark. "Touche. I was in our branch of the Special Forces, which is similar to your Army Special Forces. I put in 20 years, retired, and turned winemaker.

This was always in our family, so I just took over once I was discharged. You?"

"I am a retired Marine with my own business. I do investigate art thefts but also work with various branches of law enforcement around the world to catch murderers when they relate to those art thefts. Nice to meet you."

"Likewise. Now, let's talk about your land, Marta, and whatever else is bothering you."

Damn. He must be a mind reader.

Chapter 63

We move to the terrace, relax in the late afternoon sun, and listen as Lorenzo fills us in on my land, how and when my family acquired it, what a great businessman my great-grandfather was, how much wine we produce, how far our land extends, where my estate is from here, and more. He points to a map on the wall, with our land highlighted.

"I'm sure you have many questions, Marta. I can assure you your interests are being cared for. There is an attorney in Venice that holds your money in a trust fund. I deposit and withdraw as necessary for the business and operation. You can ask him for a complete accounting.

"I will need to know what you want to do, going forward. It's totally your call. By legal rights, you and I own equal parts in this operation. You own your own land outright. For the winery, we can continue on as we are doing, you can sell to whomever you want to, or you can try to buy me out." With that, he smiles at me.

"Goodness, I have no desire to buy you out."

"Good. You probably couldn't anyway. I love this land, creating great wines, and working with the property.

"We will take a tour of some of the land tomorrow morning. We will also stop by and look at the estate your grandmother left to you. There's only a small building left and it's in disrepair. Most of your estate consists of land. I've arranged for a van to take us up into some of the vineyards. Would that be okay?"

"That would be fantastic. We are staying at a hotel in town and can be here whenever you want."

"Nonsense. You need to stay here. Our guest house has seven bedrooms and four baths. I insist. I can have a driver fetch your things from the hotel or you can get them. Either way, you're staying here."

Clark seems to approve of this arrangement. "Thank you for your kind hospitality. I think it would be wise for us to stay here. We've had some troubles over the past few days and this way I can kind of keep an eye on things."

"Troubles? You must tell me. First, let me assure you that you will be safe. The guest house is on my main estate property, which is gated and protected by security guards."

When we look puzzled, Lorenzo explains. "You may not know how valuable of an operation this is. Any piece or part that gets into the wrong hands would not be a good thing. We just protect what is ours and then we don't have to worry.

"Now, tell me about your troubles."

Clark seems to be the spokesman and he starts at the beginning, with the music boxes. He must trust Lorenzo, because he's telling him everything. While he talks, Lorenzo listens and nods. Millie has moved to a comfortable chair and is taking a nap in the fading sun. Somehow a kitten found her lap and is dozing with her.

As the story winds down, Clark fills him in on Marcus and our fiasco from last night.

Lorenzo nods some more. "Do you have the registry you are referring to? I assume you didn't leave it at the hotel."

"I have it in my backpack and it's been with us the whole time. I wasn't about to take any chances with it. It may be nothing more than a nice old book with old family records, but we don't know at this point."

"Right. We can look at it later. My German is pretty good but sometimes old documents don't use the same German we do now. We'll figure it out, though.

"Basically, Marta, you are wondering about your grandmother, her music boxes, and her jewelry. Is that correct?"

"Yes it is. I was just curious until all this other horrible stuff started happening. Now, I don't know what to think. I really thought I knew my grandma but apparently she had quite a different life before she came to the United States.

"At this point, I'd like to know where she found these things and if they are really mine. If they are, I need to figure out what to do with them. It doesn't seem right to lock them away in a safe where no one can enjoy them. A few of the jewelry pieces I would like to keep and wear. Maybe keep one of the music boxes, as long as no one is going to steal it from me.

"I guess that's why I'm here. To put some sort of closure on Grandma's life and try to see her as she lived in this country. The rest of it does intrigue me. Like, why this registry was hidden. What's in it? Did it pertain to Grandma? I guess that's all part of finding closure on her life in Italy.

"After that, I would like to enjoy my villa in Venice several times a year. And, continue to drink our wonderful Prosecco."

Lorenzo smiles at this. "I think I can help with some of those things."

Chapter 64

Our belongings are brought from the hotel and we all settle into spacious rooms at Lorenzo's estate prior to dinner. The window in my room overlooks the vineyards, with the Dolomites in the distance. I can almost see Grandma growing up here and yet loving the city of Venice. These are two completely different yet fantastic worlds.

Clark has been on the phone most of the time while Mario has been in contact with Sam, who was called away on a family emergency.

We all convene on the terrace for drinks as both Mario and Clark fill us in on their conversations. Clark goes first.

"I've talked to Joseph, my contact at Interpol. Thomas has not been heard from or seen since the incident at your place, Mario. He could be coming here. What they do know is that he was in recent contact with Reid. Putting two and two together, it appears he was on Reid's payroll in the past. In other words, a dirty cop.

"Interpol is not sending anyone here unless we want them to. I took the liberty to talk to your guards and then filled Interpol in on your security, Lorenzo. I don't feel it's necessary for us to have any more security here right now. Reid isn't going to send his men here.

Everybody okay with that?"

We all nod in agreement.

Mario asks about his place and Clark informs him the Venice police have it covered.

Mario then relates his conversation with Sam. "He received a phone call requesting he be of assistance to a family he once worked with. When he arrived, they had not called him and had no idea who did. He arrived back in Venice a couple of hours ago and realized he had several messages that didn't come through while he was away.

"He has had a chance to look at your jewelry, Marta, and discovered some of it belonged to a royal family in Hungry or Austria. Apparently, one stamp on the back of a piece indicates a jeweler in Hungry and another is from a famous jeweler in Austria. When he made some calls to his connections in Vienna, they confirmed the markings as those of an old jewelry house in Vienna. It's still in existence and they keep records forever. It's just accessing those records that will take a day or so.

"These records will tell whom each piece was made for and when. They will also indicate if the pieces were reported stolen or lost at any time. This is good news as we will have some names and places once they get back to Sam."

"I can't believe we're that close to finding out who the jewelry belonged to or how Grandma came to have it in her possession. That is fantastic, Mario."

Lorenzo has been listening to both Clark and Mario. As he directs us into the dining room for dinner, he makes an announcement. "After dinner I have asked one of my lab assistants to join us for dessert and cordials. He speaks and reads German. His grandfather came from Germany and spoke an older version at home, so he may be able to read the German from your registry, Marta. Would that be okay with you?"

"Absolutely. It would be great if we had some idea before our trip into the vineyards and hills tomorrow. I almost forgot. We also have an old map Grandma had hidden away. I'm not sure if it means anything or not. Mario, do you still have that?"

Chapter 65

Clark has retrieved the registry and Mario the map as we meet Franz, Lorenzo's lab assistant. Clark fills him in on a little of how we came upon both, telling him we'd like to be certain of what they tell us. Lorenzo explains that I own half of this operation as well as land not far from here. Franz has been with Lorenzo for years and knows where my land is located. He looks like he could work in the vineyard all day and not break a sweat. He also appears to watch everything that's happening.

He focuses on Millie after the introductions. She asks him a question in German and his face lights up. Now they're carrying on a conversation of sorts with lots of hand gestures and smiles. Some in English; some in German. Millie explains she and her late husband used to visit friends close to where Franz grew up. They are talking about history and how it changes the world. This woman amazes me more every day.

Lorenzo has the registry and the map both laid out on a table in the den and we all gather around it. Franz looks at the map, turning it over to read what we thought might be a deed on the back side. It isn't a deed, according to Franz. "I believe it is just the description of this property. The words are somewhat faded but I believe it's referring to land not around here, but more into

Austria. According to the date, I would assume it is Austria. You could take this to an attorney, but I don't really think this is a legal document. Perhaps we will find something that cross references it."

"Darn. I do wonder why Grandma went to the trouble to hide it. Or, maybe her mother always had it in that drawer and that's just where it was kept. Still, it's odd if it's not really a deed or something important."

"Marta, keep in mind it may be important as the reference piece. I should know more once I read through the registry."

"Right. Thanks. I know we want to get an early start tomorrow morning, Lorenzo. Should we give Franz time to read through everything?"

"Great idea, if that's okay with all of you. Clark, what are your thoughts?"

Clark had been watching Franz as he was looking over the map and as he opened the first page of the registry. "I think that would be acceptable. We could leave it here in the den for Franz to access tomorrow. Franz, would you be able to make some notes depending upon what you find on each page?"

"Absolutely. I was going to suggest I write down what I translate. That way you will have it for future reference. I do have a question, though. As I opened the first page, I noticed a name. Do you know if the name Sante refers to the owner of this registry or what it might be in reference to?"

That got our attention. Clark, Mario, and I all start to speak at once. They defer to me. "We think the name Sante has something to do with my great-grandmother or her family as it isn't the maiden name of my grandmother. Nowhere do we see the Sante name listed as her father's name. So, we were making assumptions it belonged to her mother. We have several reasons to believe that; there is a large S on the door to my villa that belonged to Grandma's family, there is a large S on a couple of brooches and crests I have, and there is an S in a painting. We were hoping this registry would fill in the blanks.

"Why do you ask?"

Franz is nodding as I speak. "Well, if I remember correctly the name Sante or Santie was a ruling family of a small estate in Austria. Quite wealthy. Something is sticking in my brain about that. You see, my family had relatives living in that part of Austria, just over the border from the part of Germany where my family lived. It was a long time ago, but part of the history of that region. I need to think about that and may need to contact an uncle if I can't gain the right information from this. Would that be okay?"

Clark is the one who answers. "Why don't you see what you can get out of the registry first? Let's wait to contact your uncle."

"Sure. No problem. I'll look at this first thing in the morning and have some translation for you when you return. I can't wait to read it. I love history."

Chapter 66

We spent the entire morning touring vineyards that belonged to both Lorenzo and me, stopping only for lunch at a great little restaurant in a village. As we made our way a few kilometers further east, Lorenzo pointed to some buildings that looked as if they had seen better days. Up close, they looked worse. Much worse.

"We are now on the original property your family owned, Marta. All this land, now underneath the bramble and growth, was once farmed. There was a larger house but it has since been destroyed. These two buildings are all that remain and they are in pretty bad shape. You own this property by yourself. You'll have to decide what you want to do with it."

"You're right. There isn't much here. What do you suggest, Lorenzo? What would you do if this was yours?"

"I would have what's left of the buildings removed and convert it back into vineyards. It would take a few years to produce any fruit, but it would be better than letting it get overgrown and do nothing."

"That's kind of what I was thinking. When we get back to your place, could you put me in touch with the right people to take of that for me?"

"Yes, I can. I have some people who work for me that would be the ones to talk to or even handle the process for you. I'll introduce you."

I loved seeing the land where Grandma grew up even though no actual house still existed. Finished looking at this, I knew I would have Lorenzo's guys turn all of this back into vineyards. It just seemed right.

Mario speaks up. "Do you know the area where the ruined castle was; the one where Grandpa and Lydia found the boxes? Marta, did you happen to bring one of your grandma's maps along? That might give us a direction."

Pulling one of Grandma's maps out of my purse, Lorenzo takes a look at it, and points to a hill. "If they drew things correctly, it should have been somewhere in this direction."

Clark is out of the van looking in the direction Lorenzo pointed. "There appears to be a well-worn trail up this small hill that leads to a larger hill. It seems a little odd that it is this worn, considering the rest of this property is so overgrown. Maybe we should walk around the old buildings and then follow the trail up the hill. Millie, you don't have to come. I'm not sure how steep or how long it is. You could wait here with the van."

"Clark, my dear boy, I will most certainly come with you. I may be slow but I'm up to my ears in this adventure. Please give me your arm and lead the way."

We all smile and chuckle as Clark and Millie move around the van and start following the trail. We join in behind them. The rocky trail isn't overgrown like the rest of the land, but it's slow going in places as we make our way up it. It's further than I thought at first. Coming closer we began to see an outline of an old foundation here, too. Old, stone steps, two low walls, and a pile of rocks are all that remain. Mario walks around the outside of the base to the far corner.

"Look. Right here by all this rubble is where Grandpa and Lydia must have found the boxes. It looks like a hole of some sort was here and now partially covered."

Turning around and motioning for us to come and look at what he discovered, Mario tripped and almost fell down. "Damn. What the hell? Pardon my language, Millie."

Millie giggled and Clark quickly turned toward Mario. "What did you trip over?"

Mario looks down. "It's a body. And a shovel."

Chapter 67

Clark is the first to get to Mario. "Don't anyone touch anything. I am taking a shot of this and sending it to Interpol. It looks fairly recent."

The rest of us appear to be frozen in time. We don't move a muscle. Mario backs away and quietly says to me, "I think it's Thomas. From Interpol. I can't be certain, but it looks like him. What would he be doing here? I wonder if he followed us. He certainly knew where we were coming."

Lorenzo is looking at the trail we just came up. "I wonder if others have been here recently. Some of the larger rocks are moved off to the side. But, why? Would someone think there is still something here? Maybe we should look a little more carefully, if we can do that without looking at that body."

Millie is sitting down on one of the flat rocks and I ask her if she wants to go back down to the van. "I think I would like that, if it's okay."

"No problem. Let me walk down with you."

"You don't have to do that. I can walk down by myself. I'll be careful."

"Really, I don't mind. In fact, I'd just as soon get away from this area anyway. Let's go." I tell Lorenzo to let Mario and Clark know we are going to the van.

As we slowly make our way back down the trail, Millie asks, "Who was that? Do you think Clark knows who it is?"

"I'm not sure. I believe Mario thinks it could be Thomas, who was at his villa interviewing us. I didn't look at him."

"That poor man. I know Clark thinks he was a bad guy, but it's still too bad. What do you think he was doing here? I don't understand.

"Marta, this is getting more confusing all the time. I don't understand how everything is connected, do you? Lydia and Luigi were so nice to me. I loved being with her and I loved listening to all the stories of treasure hunting, secret hiding places, and jewels. At first, it was fun figuring out what Lydia was trying to tell you. Now, I'm tired of it all.

"Do you think Lydia knew anything about those music boxes and her jewelry?"

With Millie just ahead of me, I ask her to step aside for a second so I can bend down to move a couple of the larger rocks. That way neither of us will trip.

"Millie, I wish I could answer . . . oof." I'm cut off in mid-sentence as a strong arm grabs me around the throat and a hand covers my nose and mouth. My feet are lifted off the ground as I'm literally thrown back up against a person. With the wind knocked out of me and having trouble breathing, I try to swat my hands and kick my feet. This only makes breathing harder as someone gruffly whispers into my ear.

"Stop fighting or I will kill her and then you."

Out of the corner of my eye, I look down at the ground beside me and see Millie laying there, a reddish bump forming on her head. I want to struggle more and help Millie but I'm losing focus. Everything is blurring. Swallowing is impossible.

"Did you hear me?" The gruff voice again.

I try to nod my head and the arm eases some off my throat. At least I can swallow a little as he keeps his hand over my mouth.

"If you scream or make any noise, I will slice her throat. Then, I'll kill you and go after your friends. No one will hear anything. Got it?"

I nod and try to speak. "What, what do you want?" I sound like a sick duck.

My attacker hisses. "I want what is mine. And, I'm going to get it. You're meddling where you shouldn't be. None of this belongs to you."

As my mind and vision began to clear ever so slightly, I think to myself that I need to keep him talking. Maybe Clark, Lorenzo, or Mario will see what is happening. Yet, I don't want to endanger Millie. Poor Millie. I look again to the ground where she lays motionless.

My attacker tightens his grip. "Got the keys?"

Shaking my head, I start to speak but get brutally cut off.

"Good. The van won't start anyway." He tosses my camera on the ground, turns to the side and kicks Millie, tightens his grip on my throat even more, and continues dragging me down the trail.

"Where . . . are . . . we . . . going?" I manage to squeak out. My mind is getting fuzzy again and nothing makes sense. I'm losing it.

"First, I get what's mine. Then, I'll take care of you. They'll never find you, you meddling bitch." He eases off my throat just a little.

This clears my mind just enough for me to realize I need to do something quickly to stop him. But what? Still having a hard time breathing and swallowing, I make myself as hard to drag as possible, hoping it will take him longer to get where we're going. He tightens his grip on me and once again I find it almost impossible to breathe. This time the world is slowly going black.

The next thing I hear is a loud bang.

Chapter 68

Everything happened in slow motion after that.

My attacker stumbles and falls, taking me down with him. I end up completely underneath him, my face buried in the dirt, trying to breathe. His hand relaxes off my throat but this time I have a huge weight on top of me and a mouth full of dirt.

I hear voices in the distance and all sorts of commotion. Since I have no idea what's going on, I try to lay as still as possible. I don't know if he has friends coming to his rescue or what until I hear my name.

"Marta. Marta, I am so sorry. Clark, I think I killed Marta."

Just like that my gruff voiced attacker is lifted off me and I take in big gulps of air, coughing and choking.

"She's alive. Marta, talk to me." As I turn my head, I see Millie's shoes. Then her hands brushing dirt off my face. "Marta, are you okay? Clark, come help me. Oh dear."

With the weight off my body, Clark helps me sit up. "Just stay sitting for a minute. Do you know what happened?"

Shaking my head, I try to speak but my voice comes out hoarse and raspy.

Clark brushes some more dirt off me. "Don't speak. Here is one of our bottles of water. Drink. Or wash out your mouth. I think you may have swallowed some dirt by the looks of your face."

I look up. Lorenzo is on the phone. Mario is standing a couple of feet away with his arm around Millie. On the ground is a motionless man with a bloody shirt. What is going on?

Nodding to Clark, he helps me stand as Mario helps Millie to a seat on a nearby rock. He takes a small gun out of her hand. With an ugly bruise on her head and her hair all messed up, Millie looks worse than I feel. Worried frowns fill all their faces.

"Let's sit down and try to piece together what happened." Clark directs us all to the van as Lorenzo puts his phone in his pocket and joins us. Nodding to Clark, it's obvious he has something to tell us.

Clark starts by asking if Millie or I could tell them what happened first. I let Millie tell her part. "We were walking down the trail when something hit my head. I was looking down and stepping over big rocks on the ground so I didn't see what hit me. We were talking about Lydia and Marta's jewelry, I think. That's all I remember until . . ."

Hoarsely, I add my part. "That's right. Only I didn't see Millie get hit as I was grabbed around the throat. He must have timed it just right to get us both when we were looking down at the ground. I had a hard time breathing and things were going fuzzy. His arm was tight around my throat and I couldn't swallow. I saw Millie on the ground with a bump on her head but I couldn't focus real well. He made references to wanting what was his. Then he told me the van wouldn't start. He was dragging me and had his hand around my throat again. That's about all I remember. Until the gun shot. Or, at least it sounded like a gunshot. What was that?"

Millie nods and continues. "All of a sudden I felt someone kick me. Apparently that jolted me enough to see him dragging Marta away from me. I didn't think. I opened my handbag and pulled out my gun. Then I sat up, braced my arm on my knee like I was taught, and I pulled the trigger. I was afraid I killed you, Marta. You didn't move. I thought I aimed wrong."

"You have a gun? Oh, Millie, you didn't kill me. I am so proud of you."

Chapter 69

As it turns out, Millie and her seamstress friend had taken shooting lessons and each own a small handgun. Don't mess with these women . . .

Clark asks the obvious. "Why did you happen to have the handgun with you, Millie?"

"Oh. I always carry it with me. I even had a special handbag made by my favorite designer in Venice. He made a special pocket inside where it fits very nicely. See." Millie opens her handbag and sure enough, there is a nice pocket just for her small handgun.

We all smile. None of us can believe she had the presence of mind to actually use it. What a woman.

Clark, all business again, turns to Lorenzo. "What was your phone call about?"

"There was some trouble at my place. I'll fill you in when we return home and I have more details."

"Is everything all right?" We are all concerned.

Lorenzo smiles. "Yes. You see, Franz is more than my trusted lab assistant. He was the one who trained me in the Special Forces Division I was in. He can handle himself quite well, despite the fact that he looks older.

Now, what did you learn about the dead man at the top of the hill? And, what are we to do with both of these guys?"

"We need to wait here for a few more minutes. There should be someone from the local police who will take both of them and hold them in their morgue until Interpol can pick them up. The man at the top is definitely Thomas, who was closely associated with Reid. He must have still been on Reid's payroll and was still a dirty cop. I also shot a photo and fingerprints to my contact a few minutes ago to see who this one is.

"Millie, will you be okay if we wait here a few more minutes?"

Millie is now sitting in the van trying to fix her hair. "Of course. Does anyone have something I can use to wipe the dirt off my face and arms?"

I dig out some more wipes from my bag and then it hits me. "Wait a minute. I do remember this guy asking if I had the keys to the van and then telling me it wouldn't work anyway. What did he mean?"

Lorenzo opens the hood and sees a couple of hanging wires. "It looks like he just disconnected these. I was afraid he had cut them or destroyed something. I'm sure I can get it running. Do you remember anything else he said?"

Trying to focus, I relive those moments that seemed like hours. "He kept mumbling, or at least it sounded like mumbling, about taking what was his or what wasn't mine. I can't quite get it all straight. He called me a meddling bitch or something like that. I tried to ask questions but he told me to shut up. I couldn't breathe or really talk very well, anyway.

"I never got a good look at his face, either. He grabbed me from behind. I still don't understand how he hit Millie and grabbed me without either of us seeing or hearing him."

Millie looks up from cleaning her face. "I know. I stopped a little behind you. Remember? It was the part with more rocks. I think you were trying to move some of them out of my way."

"Right. I did bend over to move a couple of larger rocks. That must have been when he hit you and immediately grabbed me.

But, what was he doing here? Do you think he killed Thomas?"

Clark nods. "I would bet on it. We just need to figure out what they were both doing at this site. It's not like there is anything left here, right?"

Mario looks up as Clark is talking. "Wait a minute. I'm not so sure. I'm going back up to the rubble and take a look at one thing that's bothering me."

Lorenzo looks at Clark. "Why don't you stay here with Millie and Marta and I'll go with Mario? I think I know what he saw."

Chapter 70

Millie and I are sitting in the van as Clark talks to the Italian authorities about the series of events. He also puts them in touch with Interpol, who says they will have agents here within the hour. They've brought Thomas down in a body bag and put him in their van. Now they are about to do the same with the one that attacked me as Clark's phone rings.

He's nodding all the while someone is talking to him. "Thanks. That's amazing. That's the best news we've had in a long time. Thanks again."

"Clark, what is it?" I only hear part of his conversation but it seems like it could be good news.

"Well, you won't believe who this guy is. Did you get a good look at him, Marta?"

"Not really. I wanted to forget him. Why?"

"If you can, please look at his face. Tell me what you see."

Getting out of the van and cautiously approaching the man the authorities are about to zip into a body bag, I ask if I can see his face. They stop and turn his face toward me.

Gasping, I look at Clark. "It's him, isn't it? It's the guy from Grandma's hospital room, the delivery guy, and the guy from the market. I bet he's also the same guy that tried to grab Millie. Right?

Who is he?"

Clark thanks the authorities for letting me see him and directs me back to Millie. Millie has been looking around us and is now nodding her head in agreement. "Yes, that's the guy who tried to shove me into the boat. I'm glad I shot him. Oh dear. I shot someone. I killed someone. What are they going to do to me, Clark? I'm a murderer."

As realization of all the events of the past hour unfolds in Millie's brain, she becomes slightly agitated and concerned.

Clark soothes her. "Don't worry, Millie. You are not a murderer. You did shoot someone but only in self defense and to save Marta's life. No one is going to have any issue with that. In fact, once Interpol knows all about this man trying to forcibly take you into his boat they will honor you as a hero. Please don't worry. You absolutely did the right thing. We are all just glad you were here and you knew how to shoot that little handgun you carry around in your handbag. I'm still amazed by that. You are quite the woman, you know."

Millie seems to relax as Clark is talking to her.

I'm smiling as he talks to her. He has quite the way of getting her to calm down. "Okay, Clark. Who is he and what does he have to do with us?"

Clark stands up and tells Millie and me he just had confirmation on his identity. "His real name is Leo Santori but he had several aliases. He started out in the profession of small time art thief and was quite good at it; never getting caught, always escaping just before the authorities could nab him. He graduated to big time art thief and was just as successful. That's when Reid took him under his wing and perfected his skills.

"As time progressed and Reid wanted the music boxes, he put an elaborate plan together for Leo. He is indeed the delivery man you saw and most likely the man at your grandmother's bedside. There wasn't any surveillance at the hospital that caught his face. He was also the man you saw at the market, Marta, and the one who tried to get you into his boat, Millie."

"But why?"

"Well, this plan Reid had apparently included snatching Millie and holding her for ransom. That could have turned ugly if not for your quick thinking at the market, Millie. Way to go."

"Thanks. I think."

"Reid also gave him the alias of Leo Sante, convincing him he was the rightful owner of some of the music boxes and all of the jewelry. Reid dangled millions of dollars before Leo's eyes. Leo was determined to get back from Marta what he thought was rightfully his. He would have gone to any lengths to get his hands on it. He was that greedy. He even outsourced some of his dirty work, just like he learned from Reid. That included Marcus, the driver, and a few other unsavory characters.

"One problem Leo had was that Reid was getting impatient. Very impatient. Reid kept upping the time frame for Leo and Leo started getting careless in his haste. No idea why Reid was so impatient. But, that's why things really started happening after your grandmother died, Marta."

Clark pauses to see Mario and Lorenzo coming down the path carrying a large piece of stone.

"What on earth are you going to do with that stone?"

Mario and Lorenzo grin at each other. "Wait until you see what it is."

Chapter 71

Bringing it closer for us to get a better look, Mario points to a date carved into the stone. We can almost make out the date 1870 or something close to that, depending on the erosion and wear.

I look at Mario. "Great. But what does it mean and why are you so excited about it?"

"The date might be important. But, what I first saw that grabbed my attention was this worn crest on the other side. Look. It says 'Royal House of Sante'. This means the Sante name was connected to your great-grandmother somehow, Marta."

Lorenzo nods in agreement. "We need to get back to my place. Many things happened since we left. One has to do with this stone. Let's get back and talk to Franz and the others."

"Others?" Clark isn't sure he likes the sound of that. "What others?"

"Remember I told you about some trouble that Franz handled? Let's go see what he has to say."

Driving back to Lorenzo's place, we are all silent. Two more men are dead and it still has to do with my music boxes and jewelry. When will this ever stop? I'm so tired of thinking about who is good and who is bad. I just want this whole nightmare to be over.

Millie has dozed off, thank goodness. I can't believe the spirit and fight of that woman, especially given her age. She's quite the individual.

Clark is texting and emailing someone. Mario is silent. We've had quite the last couple of days.

Approaching the gate to Lorenzo's long driveway, we see it's already open. Driving closer, several black, cars are parked by the front steps with a couple of beefy men standing at the front door. What the hell is going on?

One of the beefy men opens our van's doors and tells us we need to talk to some people inside. I sure hope it's not more trouble. This is bizarre, yet Lorenzo seems to take it all in stride.

We're all quickly ushered into the den, where Clark greets one of the men sitting with Franz. "Charles, how good to see you. How is Paris and how is your lovely wife? But, this can't be good. You only come when there's a major problem. Let me introduce everyone and then we need to know what's going on."

Introductions made, we're all sitting down, coffee is served, and Charles stands up. "You probably all know pieces and parts of this bizarre tale, but let me start from the beginning. Or, at least the beginning of Interpol's and Scotland Yard's involvements."

Charles relates the tale of Reid and his stolen art business, adding in more details than we first knew. I can tell he's leaving out most of the grisly ones. Still, we discover Reid is an evil man who doesn't mind murder and torture. Charles covers the attempts of Marcus and Thomas to steal whatever they could, all at Reid's direction.

When Clark relates the events of our afternoon, Charles smiles at Mille and tells her he approves of her shooting Leo and tells her she is a fantastic shot. She will indeed be heralded as a hero. Millie beams at this.

The mood is somber as we all soak up this information. I look around the room and see Clark is the only one on edge. I'm not sure why. "Charles, is there something you're not telling us?"

"Clark, you know me so well. Yes, there is one last thing. I want to be sure everyone can handle this." Charles surveys each one of us as we nod in turn.

Chapter 72

Charles continues. "Remember how I mentioned Reid seemed to be upping his game, asking Leo and his cohorts to get the music boxes to him more quickly than before? Well, apparently that wasn't even enough for him. He made an appearance here this morning."

A collective gasp fills the den. We all ask questions at once and Charles holds up his hand.

"Just a minute. Let me finish, please.

"Yes, Reid was here. I have no idea how he made it past your security, Lorenzo. He's good. Unfortunately, he unsuccessfully tried to poison one of your guard dogs. He'll be okay. Then, Reid entered through a window and made his way to where Franz was reading your registry, Marta. All the time, undetected. He would have killed Franz had Franz not seen a reflection in one of the glass decanters on the side table.

"Franz still has his skills and fortunately still carries a weapon.

"Reid is dead."

Another gasp is heard. Once more, questions flow. Once more, Charles holds up his hand. We become silent.

"Yes. Reid is dead. He has been positively identified. His mansion on the outskirts of London is being thoroughly investigated as we speak. He had quite the security system there, with explosives rigged in some of the rooms as well. Scotland Yard's bomb squad has disarmed everything.

"There is just one more thing. Reid was dying. In fact, he had a hospital of sorts set up in his home. Scotland Yard surprised the physician there and he is cooperating fully. The physician tells us Reid didn't have long to live, which could explain his haste.

"Now, let me hear your questions." He looks to Clark.

"Any idea why he was fixated on Marta's and Mario's music boxes? Did he have what he thought of was the entire collection, minus theirs?"

"We know he has several. We think he found out about your grandmother's boxes through a contact in San Francisco. Shortly, I want all of you to look at Reid's face. I need to know if you have ever seen him before. I'm sorry and I know it's a gruesome thing to ask of you. Especially you, Millie, but it needs to be done. We have to be sure we tie up all the loose ends."

We all nod and Millie speaks first. "I don't care what he looks like as long as he is dead. He's caused enough grief for all of us. Especially Marta. Lydia wouldn't have liked that. Let me see him."

Charles chuckles under his breath. He's getting to see the spunky side of Millie we have come to know and love. "Just a few more minutes, Millie. The coroner is getting him ready for us to see. As I said, he's already been positively identified.

"As for the fixation on these music boxes, we assume it was because he found out about them and then wanted to get his hands on them. It seems his past thefts follow that same pattern. He hears of something he wants and puts all his energy and resources into getting that item. It shows in his extensive collection of stolen art, antiquities, and artifacts. A couple pieces are from a gallery in Vienna. They will be glad to know they're getting those returned. Same with the rest of the stolen pieces once we can identify where most of them came from originally.

"Other questions?"

"How did he know Grandma? He had his man, Leo, in her hospital room before she died. I don't think she knew Leo or Reid, for that matter, but I guess I need to look at his face before I can say that for certain. I'm just having a hard time connecting all the dots."

Franz, who has been quiet until now, speaks up. "When we are finished with the coroner, I want to tell you what is in your grandmother's registry, Marta. That might shed a little more light on things. But I want to wait for right now. I've spoken to Charles about it and he agrees. Right, Charles?"

"Yes. I'll get out of your hair and take Reid's body and then you can all relax and learn some more history of your family."

Chapter 73

The coroner enters and has a brief discussion with Charles and Clark, letting them know we can look at the body prior to it being loaded into his van.

Clark comes to me. "Marta, I want you to come outside with me and look at Reid. I know this is difficult, but it's important you take a good look at his face. It's necessary or I wouldn't ask you to do this. I want to know if he is someone your grandmother ever talked to, to your knowledge. You can tell me what you see or ask me questions. But, don't say anything to anyone else until everyone has looked at him. I want to know all of your impressions but I don't want you to influence anyone. Does that make sense?"

Nodding, I follow Clark, Charles, and the coroner to his van in the driveway. There is a raised gurney with a covered body on it. The coroner looks at me for approval and lifts the cover off of his face. As I take the first look, the world spins as disbelief and shock register. Spinning faster and faster, I have trouble standing and grab Charles for support. With my mouth hanging open, sputtering, I look at Clark with questions written all over my face.

He can tell I'm about to lose it. "Marta, what is it? What do you see? Have you seen him before? Come. Let's sit down. You're as white as a ghost. Something's very wrong."

I stumble as I turn away, and Clark and Charles both reach out to catch me. I can't breathe. Buzzing fills my ears. I'm pretty sure I'm going to throw up. They help me to a bench by the front steps. I'm sweating and shaking. Clark is concerned by my reaction.

"What the hell, Marta? Who do you think that is?" Charles has grabbed a glass of water from somewhere. "Drink this and then put your head between your knees before you pass out."

Instead, I drain the glass and try to stand up. "I need to look at him again. I need to be absolutely certain. It's been a long time. Oh my God."

Charles and Clark look at each other with concerned faces but each takes my arm as I unsteadily walk to the body. Ready to catch me if I fall, Clark takes my face in his hands. "Marta, take a good look and then we need to talk. Can you do that?"

Nodding once again, I turn and look at the face of Reid. Turning to the coroner, I take a deep breath and ask, "Can you let me see behind his right ear? Is there a large strawberry shaped birthmark?"

The coroner moves his ear and sure enough the birthmark is still there. I blink long and hard, inhaling, trying to breathe, attempting to focus.

Then I look away. The world is still spinning but at least I don't think I'll lose my lunch. Hesitantly, I look at Clark and Charles and take another deep breath. "Okay. I think I can talk now. Have you run DNA on him? Do you know what his real name is? What do you know about him? Are you sure this is the one behind all the thefts and murders?"

Charles has helped me back to the bench and both he and Clark are sitting beside me. By the looks on their faces, I can tell they are wondering about my questions.

"Yes, we are positive about the thefts and murders. We have his fingerprints on file but DNA will take some time to come back. What can you tell us about him? Anything would be helpful. Please, take your time. I know this is difficult based on your reactions, but we need to know what you see."

Taking another deep breath and exhaling, I look at Clark and then at Charles. "I can't believe I'm going to say this.

I'm positive the man on the stretcher is my father. The birthmark confirmed it for me."

Chapter 74

First, you could hear the proverbial pin drop. Even the birds seemed to have stopped singing. Then, everything is a blur. Once they're sure I'm not going to pass out, they leave me on the bench.

Charles is on the phone. Clark is on the phone. Mario and Millie make their way to the terrace once they both verify they have never seen him before.

I'm still dazed. I'm confused. I'm furious. Emotions overrun me. I'm not sure I can stand up.

Lorenzo's chef comes out and helps me stand. Then he walks with me to the terrace where he serves me a shot of whiskey and a flute of Prosecco. "Drink." Nodding, I look at him and follow his command. Then he asks if I want a sedative or want to lie down. Mario asks what he can do for me. Millie just sits and pats my knee.

The whole scene is surreal. I can hear but can't find my voice. Everything happens in slow motion and yet whizzes by so fast. I feel like I'm a bystander at some odd play.

Finally, after what seems like days if not weeks, we are all once again gathered together. Charles and Clark tell us they can fill us in on a little more. "Based on your identification, Marta, we've compared Reid's fingerprints to those of your father on record at the university. DNA will confirm beyond a doubt, but we are fairly certain he is your father. We'll know more once we piece his life together.

"What we can conclude, based on what Franz found, is that your father knew of the music boxes and the jewelry. He either fell into it or your grandmother confided in him early on, before she knew what he was up to. Perhaps later she figured it out and that's why she didn't say anything. We'll probably never know that. We'll also never know how long he was treasure hunting and stealing, under the guise of research.

"I'm so sorry you had to learn your father was not a nice person, Marta. He fooled a lot of people. We're also guessing your mother probably had no knowledge of his second life. Or, maybe she found out and that's why their plane disappeared. It's apparent he wasn't on it when it went down. Again, speculation is all we have.

"This will all take time to sort out. And, I'm sure your mind will digest all this for quite some time to come, Marta. I know it's easy for me to say, but you should try to remember him before all of this came to light.

"For now, his collection of art is all being returned to its rightful owners. Anything left over and anything made from the sale of his mansion will go to you, Marta."

This makes me sit up and gasp. "What do you mean?"

"You are his only heir. Don't read a lot into this and don't make any hasty decisions, okay?"

"But, I'm the heir of a thief and a murderer. I don't exactly have warm, fuzzy feelings about that."

"Give it some time. You have good friends to help you through this. And, now Franz will fill you in on what he found in the registry."

All eyes turn to Franz.

Chapter 75

Three days later we are sitting on the terrace at Mario's villa; Clark, Mario, Sam, Millie, and me. Charles has gone back to Paris or wherever his main office is located. Lorenzo and Franz are back at the winery. Looking around at everyone, we are all in our own world. Thinking about the past events.

Has it really only been three days?

I've learned so much. Looking towards the Heavens once more, I utter a silent prayer and a thanks to Grandma. It seems she was trying to keep me safe and at the same time lead me toward the secrets she discovered both long ago and in her recent years.

I've gained a new respect for her as well. She was always prepared and apparently she was preparing for my future. Only I didn't know it.

And, I've come up with more questions. Some of which will never be answered. I wonder when she knew what he was up to. She had to have suspicions. I also wonder when she really knew what she had in the jewelry and music boxes. Guess I'll never know that either.

As for Reid, I wonder if he knew it was me. There's no way I can think of him as my father. I wonder if he would really have murdered Millie or me for that matter.

I'm processing and sorting out all the discoveries. I am pretty sure everyone else is doing the same thing. Sam is the first to speak.

"Marta, you have some decisions to make about your jewelry and the music boxes. I'm not suggesting you do anything in haste, but you need to make sure you have a reliable safe either here or in San Francisco. And, you need to get everything insured. That needs to be done immediately. I have all the appraisals for you."

Nodding, I agree. "Sam, will you please relate what you found out about my jewelry to all of us again? And, what it means in the scope of things. I know I heard it . . . but I don't think I really understood it."

"Certainly. All of the jewelry, the tiara, and the music boxes belonged to your great-grandmother's family. Deciphering the jeweler's stamps and combining those with what we know of the history in those areas, everything surely had been passed down for generations in her family. Your great-grandmother came from royalty. According to what Franz found in your family registry about her lineage, this was legitimate royalty at that time.

"The painting in your villa of the woman wearing the tiara was your great-grandmother. For some reason she downplayed her royal connection, or at least didn't lead with it. We'll never know why. Just like we'll never know why your great-grandfather didn't seem to embrace that. Could have been the times; could have been his own personal thoughts. At any rate, you are a descendant of what was a royal family. The stone Mario and Lorenzo found at the site of the old castle was probably her way of letting people know the castle held some significance.

"What does this mean for you? Again, according to what Franz found in the registry, you do own land beyond the vineyards you already knew about. It was deeded from one royal family to yours. Your attorney will have a better idea if it is still yours or reverted back to some country or whatever.

"The music boxes are exactly what Clark had discovered. They are real and they did belong to royalty, also. It turns out some of the ladies they were given to were related to your ancestors.

Legally, they and the jewelry are all yours. You should take some time and decide what you want to do with all of it. If and when you want recommendations, I would be glad to help you. I think Clark will agree.

"There is one more thing I discovered in amongst all your jewelry. There is an interesting gold piece that could have been an old coin, a really ancient coin. Preliminary inspection tells me it's worth a great deal. At any rate, it's interesting and if you like, I can look into it further for you. But, you might want to consider turning it into a pendant for a necklace regardless of its worth. It's that unique. It would be a great way to remember your grandmother."

Smiling, I tell Sam, "Great idea, Sam. Thanks. I would like that and would like for you to make the pendant and necklace for me."

"Sam, please let me see it." Clark reaches for the gold piece Sam found in the bottom of the box. Turning it over and looking at it closely, Clark asks Sam, "Did you do any research on this?"

"Not beyond the preliminary. I really didn't have time. But, the markings tell me it's quite old. Why? What do you think, Clark?"

"I agree. I'd bet it's real and old. And, why wouldn't it be? It was in with everything else that's genuine. Marta, this might have some real historical significance as well as being a part of your family. I would have Sam do some more looking at it and then turn it into a necklace. You could have quite a special piece here. Take care of it."

Handing the gold piece back to Sam, Clark then relays more of what Franz found. "That was quite the family registry. You will now be able to trace some of your ancestors with the names and dates of births they recorded. That, in itself, is amazing.

"Sam is correct. The additional land may or may not still be yours. Your attorney can sort through all of that. Everything else is yours, as Sam mentioned. Interpol, the FBI, Scotland Yard, and everyone else agree. As the mansion and estate in London are sold, that amount will be yours as well.

"Marta, you are a very wealthy woman."

Millie giggles, takes a bow, and waves a finger at me. "Oh dear. Do we need to start calling you by your highness or courtesy when you enter a room?"

We all chuckle, especially at her gestures. As usual Millie can break up a somber mood. Thank goodness for her.

"Millie, you are my hero in all of this. I can't thank you enough for being a friend to my grandma and for saving my life."

She smiles. "And, to think I almost killed you. It's a good thing I have perfect aim."

&pilogue

Somewhere in San Francisco three men sit around a table in a dark room at the back of a restaurant drinking wine.

"I can't believe Reid is dead, and that bitch, his daughter, isn't. How many people screwed up? Whom can we trust, now?

"Did anyone get the coin or was that lost, too?"

About the Author

WENDY VANHATTEN is a published author, editor-in-chief for "Prime Time Living Magazine," wine, food, and travel editor for "WEMagazine," and travel enthusiast. She has taught writing at the college level, writing workshops, and is affiliated with Bay Area Travel Writer Organization, http://www.batw.org/.

Her children's books, the *Max and Myron* series, teach children to read while developing good character traits.

Travel advice and photos are updated weekly on her blog at www.travelsandescapes.blogspot.com. Her books are available online at Amazon or from her website, www.wendyvanhatten.com.

Additional Titles by Wendy VanHatten

My Life, The Sequel: A Girlfriend's Guide to Personal Success

When the Cat Speaks ... Listen, A purr ... fectly good way to enjoy life

Dad's Hidden Box

Champagne Lies

MAX & MYRON SERIES
by Wendy VanHatten and R David Kryder with illustrations by Corie Barloggi
 Max and Myron Learn Please and Thank You Max and Myron, My First Day of School
 Max and Myron I'm Sorry, Please Forgive Me Max & Myron Learn Please Don't Tease
 Max & Myron Learn Big and Small, Short and Tall

The Authorship Journey: A profitable adventure?
by Wendy Vanhatten, Ginger Marks, Misty Taggart, and Tracee Gleichner

Available on Amazon.com and fine bookstores everywhere.